Midnight Song
Quest for the Vanished Ones

Midnight

Quest for the Vanished Ones

Song

Jamie Sams

introduced by José Argüelles

BEAR & COMPANY
SANTA FE, NEW MEXICO

I dedicate this book to my spiritual sister, Molly Malone, who showed me the way, and also to my spiritual sister, Linda Wuensche, who has walked it with me.

Library of Congress Cataloging-in-Publication Data
Sams, Jamie, 1951-
   Midnight song: quest for the vanished ones/by Jamie Sams.
      p.   cm.
   ISBN 0-939680-49-1: $9.95
   1. Sams, Jamie, 1951-   . 2. Mediums—United States—Biography.
3. Occultism—United States.   I. Title.
BF1283.S29A3 1988
133.9'1'0924—dc19
[B]   88-4983
                                                                     CIP

Bear & Company
P.O. Drawer 2860
Santa Fe, NM 87504

Design & Illustration: Kathleen Katz
Cover Photography: Robert Boissiere
Cover Illustration: James Finnell
Typography: Copygraphics, Inc.
Printed in the United States of America by R.R. Donnelley
9 8 7 6 5 4 3 2 1

— Contents —

— *Acknowledgments* —

Special thanks to my Spiritual Family for their love and support and mutual processing during the writing of this book. Leslie, Mimi, Barbara, Yannina, Arrianna, Cheryl, and Nannette, the first circle. The second opening, Annie, Rod, Hawk, Carol, Gary, Barb, Bodhi, Diann, Alan, Alaina, Cliff, Mike, Heidi, Ward, Candace, Jimmy, Mark, Audrey, Linda, Ralphie, Liberty, Tim, Linda, Hardy, Barb, Trush, Jason, Donna, Steve G., Suzanne, Dave, Yvonne, Jeff, Joan, John, Vickie, Roxanne, Cindy, Edith, Mary, Clarissa, Pooder, Jody, Diane, Judith, Jacquie, Bobby, Michele, Wendy, Daria, Enid, Adrianne, Vince, Ronnie, Wheeler, Helene, Floyd, Neva, David, Judy, Pam, Ronnie, Yon, Margo, Phil, Marita, John, Sue, Eric, Colleen, George, Val, Kathleen, Jeni, Claire, and Ulli.

You have each given me a piece to my personal puzzle and I love you for it. I have grown and changed and been so very blessed for having known you all. Thank you for the tears, the laughter, the music, the challenges, the growth, and the love. As the Tibetan says, "There is the scent of heaven here; may you never be the same again."

To Bear & Company goes my deep gratitude for the completion of this book. In my typically Texas way. . . the "Grin 'n Bearettes" get my hugs and giggles!

— *Foreword* —

First of all, Jamie Sams is an artist, and as anyone really knows, an artist worth his or her salt is a channel. How else does good art come about if it isn't channeled?

Socrates spoke of the divine madness, and romantic poets have ever proclaimed the virtues of "inspiration." Long before and long after the philosophers and poets, shamans entered into trance and received the inspiration—the in-breathing—of the divine. What is this inspiration if not the process that nowadays we call channelling? And the "muses" responsible for this inspiration—who are they if not the fourth dimensional entities who watch and guide the spiritual development of humankind through the divinely bestowed gifts of vision, healing, and art?

Leonardo da Vinci wrote in his notebooks about his technique of throwing a sponge of paint on the wall. Gazing at the dripping spots and splotches left by the sponge, he would enter a revery. Visions, designs, and plans would come to him. What da Vinci ultimately developed from this technique was not only memorable art, but futuristic visions that ranged from hydraulics and wave motion to helicopters and anatomy.

This points to another ability of the visionary artist/channel: to have foreknowledge of what is to come. The artist/channel consciously or unconsciously uses the physical third-dimensional body as an instrument to divine, through a process of resonant transduction, what is available in the fourth dimension—or even dimensions beyond. This process is resonant because the vibratory field of the individual is attuned to the resonant overtones that carry information from other dimensions. It is transduction because it involves a stepping up or stepping down of energy or information.

The attuned visionary operates through an information bank reposited within the whole of his or her own biopsychic being. When truly sensitive to the nature and conditions of the times, the attuned visionary will marvelously and capably bring in needed information so that humanity might see its next possible steps. At the end of his life, Sir Francis Bacon channelled his artful fantasy, *The New Atlantis,* which in reality describes a mystic vision of society following the age of materialism. Likewise, through his unique "infernally il-luminated" printing methods, William Blake cast in mythic light the architects of reason, and foresaw the coming return of "heaven" through a superior engagement of the senses.

Our current era is one in which the phenomenon of chan-nelling has become exceedingly popular. Why? Well, for one thing, rational methods are rapidly being exhausted, and more immediate and whole-patterned information is needed. Secondly, channeling is not just the gift of weird shamanic misfits, but the birthright of humanity. The popularity of chan-nelling is a harbinger of our future collective evolutionary development.

Then there is the content of contemporary channelling. If you look at much of the information that is being channelled, it is clear that today's psychics are being challenged and con-fronted by extraterrestrial entities who have an acute concern for the condition of our planet. Whether you want to believe, like C.G. Jung, that UFOs are projections of the collective un-conscious, or that there are actually galactic witnesses hovering within the auric field of planet Earth, the fact is that the extra-terrestrial phenomenon is a potent evocation of a spirituality which is otherwise lacking in the official codes of modern life.

The pervasive contemporary presence and message of the UFOs seems to carry a multiple signal. They are saying to us: 1) your planet is in trouble; 2) we are multidimensional and so are you, but your present belief system doesn't allow that, so we seem threatening to you; 3) the fact that you are able to perceive us, and experience us at all, demonstrates that in ac-tuality you are also multidimensional; 4) therefore we are a reminder that the way out of your present planetary crisis and into the future is to acknowledge and accept again your own multidimensionality.

It is into this boiling stew of individual search and planetary crisis that Jamie Sams' story unfolds. In the best visionary manner, Sams *arts* her vision into a story that allows the reader to identify and become immersed in her world—without knowing why. Thus, it is for a very good reason that Jamie Sams suggests that the reader consider this book to be a novel. Nothing is assumed or given, and it is the reader who has to put the puzzle-pieces together. As a result, *Midnight Song* reads like both a mystery and high adventure.

What slowly and erratically unravels is the story of one woman's coming into her own as a psychic. This could be, and easily is, the story of everywoman and everyman dumped out at the end of history, coming into her or his own as an evolving multidimensional being. It is not a pretty story. The psychic gift that is already ours is covered by the accumulated misperceptions of hundreds, if not thousands, of years of living an increasingly one-dimensional existence. To shatter this miasma of fear and misperception is painful and frightening, yet it must be done.

Operating on surrender and transcendental trust, Jamie Sams is able to break through the misperceptions. Extraterrestrial, multidimensional contact is made—not necessarily in a sensational manner, but with great surprise and provocation. Though she presents critical information about the actual nature of our planet and ourselves, this information takes on even more meaning because it is set in the eerie, poetic context of a personal journey, a private storm.

When you read this book, savor its gritty flavor and then consider your own commitment to multidimensional living. The cost is your own attachment to one-dimensional perceptions. Let us hope that Jamie Sams' *Midnight Song* makes it easier for you to cross the boundary into the greater life of the universe.

JOSÉ ARGÜELLES
Boulder, Colorado
Mystic Column, North American Plate
12 Cauac 5 Ceh, Northern Year of the Sorcerers of Harmony
March 8, 1988

— *Preface* —

I have been very fortunate to always have the capacity to believe. "To believe in what?" you may well ask. Well, to believe that all things are pregnant with possibilities and magic. My life has been filled with this faith since I mentally lifted a sofa several feet off the ground at the age of three. Much to my great shock, others did not believe that they could do the same thing, and therefore they did not.

The time has come for each of us, in our own unique and curious ways, to begin to recapture the magic of our own divine natures—to live that mythical, mystical lifestyle that we have forced beyond the veil. I have walked a crooked pathway for all my years and have made peace with the fact that it could take a while for the world to regain this belief again.

The psychic facet of my existence could be called "The Life and Bizarre Times of Jamie Sams," since it has been a comedy of errors in many respects. My journey began in the buckle of the Bible Belt—a world that was not ready for the strangeness of a psychic child. The haunting memories of being in two worlds at the same time, and of not understanding why no one else could see or hear what I did, still remain.

I was accused of daydreaming in the first grade and, as I had begun school early for my age, my teachers wanted to hold me back a year. I was seeing other beings in the room with me, and was going "out of my body" with them to locations in which I was taught how to meld into a society where my fellow beings were different. I was also shown many future events, and my knowledge of these events never failed to confuse, frighten, or dismay the adults around me. I was accused of cheating when I psychically saw through playing cards, and was punished severely by a great aunt for my natural capacity to "know."

The trauma I experienced on several occasions became a hidden blessing, because it drove me deeper into my internal "safe space," and heightened my gifts. When I was two, I burned myself by falling into a floor furnace. The pain, in some way, forced me out of my body and allowed me to experience and remember colors that I had never seen before. These were the colors of the energy that we now call the aura. I learned to harness these energies and to propel them into space, thus discovering how to move objects through telekinesis.

I was sexually molested when I was nine years old, and the resulting shock of this experience became the catalyst for bringing me closer to my guardian angel and to the Creator. From a place of hurt and shame, I gained compassion and love for my fellow beings on a deep level. I began to understand that a force within me was stirring, and that that force was pure and powerful. It was the force of remembering—remembering that I had trod this pathway before, and that there was great joy in regaining the hope, and the power of love, to overcome all obstacles. I knew that I had created this pathway to jolt me into remembering.

The ancients called this the left-hand pathway, due to the duress it creates for those individuals who follow it in order to temper the sword of truth that dwells within us all. This truth cuts through our fears and our self-created demons, so that we may rise like the phoenix from the ashes of our shattered personal myths—the myths about who and what we are—to find the glory of our connection to the Source.

The extraterrestrials call that Source G.O.D.—the Generator Of Dimensions. I have experienced many of these dimensions and have, in my growing, come to know that it is a privilege to be here on this beautiful Earth, where we have been given the greatest gift of all. This gift is the ability to be co-creators of our universe with all other life forms, to decide if we want the magic or the pain, and then to see the pain as something that has served us in our growth. Transmuting pain into joy is a form of alchemy or magic, since magic is, in the definition I have come to know, merely a change in consciousness.

I have walked this path "apparently alone" for a long while.

Now there are millions who are willing to tap into this force that has belonged to them forever. I have touched the stars with my mind, held the Earth in my heart, and allowed my eyes to see the sun dawning on the purple dunes of Mars. I have traveled through time to seek the vanished ones—the ancients that colonized our Earth—and met them in the physical world high in the Andes.

How and why did I do this? Because I believed I could, and because I desired it more than life itself. To quote Albert Einstein, "I only did it because it was fun!"

I haven't changed anyone's name in this book, nor have I tampered with the sequence of events, or with any of the particulars, because it is all true, all verifiable, and frankly I don't care if anyone believes me or not. My life has been bizarre and I love it that way. I'll never let it be said of me that I lived an amateur life.

You can do this too, if you believe in the magic you can create, and if you love yourself enough to try. Journey with me and feel the stirring in your own soul as you touch the truth within yourself. This book is only an energy key to the door to the future that you will create for yourself and for all of us. We are the heirs to the knowledge of the universe, and we are blessed.

Blessed Be!

JAMIE SAMS

— *Note From The Author* —

All the events in this book are true. If it makes you, the reader, more comfortable to consider this book a novel, *be my guest.*

— *One* —

Thunderclouds rolled across the Andes, engulfing Machu Picchu. The last tourist train was gone. Shooting pangs from the torn muscle in my leg nagged me as the final train for workers and students — the Indio train — prepared to leave. It was full to overflowing. Jostling for room, the natives squabbled over space outside or on the caboose.

A two-mile walk on the tracks in the pouring rain faced me. The pueblo of Aguas Calientes and its meager hostel seemed worlds away. The train track would be safe enough to walk once the Indio train was gone. No others would come until morning. The sun had vanished with the storm, and what little light remained was dissipating behind the two-mile-high peaks above me.

Looking down at my soaked socks and sneakers, I realized that my down parka was drenched, with rainwater seeping into the clothing beneath. The air was so thin that I constantly gasped for oxygen. "What in the name of heaven am I doing here?" I thought. "Peru in the dead of winter. Am I totally crazy?" Visions arose of hot July sunshine baking the California beaches. "There are a lot of places where I could be if I hadn't agreed to follow my heart. Destiny seems like a rather empty word now, doesn't it?" I mused.

Catching myself as the first whistle sounded, I studied the faces of the once-proud Inca nation. The woodgrainy faces and undernourished bodies hit me. Torn muscle, cold, rain, and all, I was blessed. I didn't have to live in their world. Their only lifeline was this railroad track — a tiny black ribbon snaking through the sleeping Andes.

Time had frozen in this part of creation; the customs had not changed for hundreds of years. Many of the mountain people didn't even speak Spanish. Quechua, the Incan mother tongue, had been only gradually replaced since the

1500s. This was 1984! I felt as if I were in a time warp. High above me on the right was the last Inca holdout — Machu Picchu. To the left of the ruins was the Royal Inca Road. I knew what had happened there from the visions I had seen in my mind's eye. Something was missing. I hadn't had the strength to climb the big mountain to the Temple of the Moon because of the accident and my leg. "Had I failed?" I asked myself. Was the big mountain really cavernous? Was the hole I had found really the answer to ancient records that had been hidden for thousands of years?

I cringed at the thought of my options: either returning to the tiny hostel with no hot water, or trying to climb the hillside to the mineral pools as my leg swelled with alarming rapidity. At that moment, a tiny hand touched my elbow. I looked down into the shining face of a little girl. "Come with me, Señorita, your leg is bad. Hurry, we must get on the train! We will ride to the pueblo; you mustn't walk."

It was Ruth. Although she had entered her teens, Ruth exuded a radiant innocence which made her appear childlike. When we met the day before, she had been selling jewelry her father had made. Since my Spanish is excellent, we had become fast friends. I hobbled behind her as she shouted, like a fourteen-year-old drill sergeant, for the people to make room.

The next-to-last car had a space for me outside on the stairs, but no handhold. Three other people pushed up behind me. My face pressed against the door between the cars, and I realized that fifteen people were crowded into the space in front of the door, inside the train. The cars were filled to triple capacity, and should the door open from the inside, we would all fall off. Frightened because I had no secure holding rail, I insisted on getting down.

Ruth began yelling in Quechua for the people to let us ride in the two spaces allowed by the step. Like the Red Sea, the wall of people parted. She pushed me to the top step, which had one handhold, and took the bottom one herself. This lower step had two handholds, which she could use to brace me on. The train would have to pass through two tunnels carved from living rock — the body of the mountain — on its two-mile jaunt to the pueblo. I had walked through them often in the past two days, and it immediately dawned on me how close their sides were to the train. As the whistle blew and the train picked up steam, I babbled my concern to Ruth. "Don't worry, Señorita, I will protect you," she comforted.

I looked at the door in front of me, with its bulging mass of people, and saw that the hinge was broken on the side closest to my only holding rail. The door buckled outward. Clearance in the tunnels was at times as narrow as twelve inches between the train and the wall of stone. I couldn't get comfortable enough to feel safe. Ruth's body literally held me in position. Turning my head to the left, I saw the first tunnel rapidly approaching. Halfway down was a huge rock which the cars in front of us, even without extra passengers on their steps, were just barely missing. I screamed at Ruth to look. We pressed our bodies as close to the door as possible, and for one brief but eternal moment, I prayed. Engulfed in the darkness, I mumbled, "Oh God, please keep this tiny girl from harm's way. Please save her life. . . keep us safe!" A light went on in my head like a frame from some horror movie. My life flashed before me, and instantly I remembered the day before.

My bus had descended that day from the ruins of Machu Picchu to the train depot below. I began walking the train back to Aguas Calientes alone. The Vilacanota River, its banks covered with wild lilacs, bubbled with whitewater rapids. River rocks glowed pink from the setting Peruvian sun. On the tracks above the river embankment, I stood for one long moment, trying to drink in the beauty of the other shore. High across the embankment rose the peaks which descended from Machu Picchu. Indians filed down the majestic, crater-like Inca Trail, chewing their coca leaves against the cold. Tiny women, between four- and five-feet tall, carried their loads in brightly woven rebozos. Some had children pressed to their breasts. Others spun llama wool on a top-like device, and still others carried bundles of vegetables. Each woman wore a skirt and hat representing her home province, and the men were just as colorful.

I hadn't thought it strange that they were coming across the river to get to the tracks; I just supposed they were coming to the pueblo for market. But drawing closer to the village, I noticed some of the people pointing at me and whispering. I knew they saw hundreds of Europeans and Americans flock to the ruins each year. I was no different, but I felt a little bit curious when I overheard one lady say, "The Madonna is coming, the Madonna is coming." I glanced behind me to see if some religious procession were going on behind me, but the tracks were bare. As I entered the village, a group of nearly fifty people awaited me. The adults hung back; the children in front began to giggle. I smiled and began to pass them on my way up the trail leading to the hostel.

One of the children pushed a ten-year-old boy in front of me. He stumbled, and I grabbed him to keep him from falling. Noticing his club foot, I was suddenly angry at the cruelty with which they had treated him. As I checked to see if he was all right, he smiled and grasped my hand. His lips parted and he stuttered, "Señorita, please. . .make me well!"

I couldn't believe my ears. Was this a trick? Who had told these people that I could heal anyone? As my shock and fear receded, I heard myself answer that I would try. I laid my hands on his leg and manipulated the acupressure points. This had been successful on a couple of occasions back in California, and I knew that the force of love could heal. But why me? Who was I to try to use these divine gifts? I was no lost Inca goddess. I was only a mortal, fragile, human being who loved the world's people. I heard a Voice say, "Who better then? Who but another that has seen pain should be the bearer of hope?"

I spent many hours, long into the night, seeing all the villagers who asked for help. Some had come to be healed, some to get a glimpse of hope for the future. I was powerless to refuse. I laughed and cried with them, and held their babies, knowing that some would die. I told them to look only to their Creator, and not to me, for miracles. I lived a lifetime in those hours. Most of all, I grew a hundred years in wisdom. If that had been my time to die, I knew that I would have died in peace. Mission accomplished; love had been shared. I believed that those hours lived on in the hearts of my new friends, and that they would remember the "Americana" who helped them laugh.

As I completed this memory from yesterday and returned to the present situation, I found myself hanging onto the outside of a screaming train with a tiny girl supporting my pain-wracked body. In that moment, I understood Ruth's love for me. She was returning the gratitude of her people with strength and bravery. I was ashamed. I had been the fearful one. I had been weak and alone in this strange land. "Oh, Great Spirit, don't let her die," I mentally screamed. Why wasn't I the one on the outside? Was this the end? Or was it a new level of understanding about people and how vulnerable we really are? My mind raced through this split second of time as though it were infinity. How had this all begun?

This voyage of mine into "terra infirma" had led me to the magical mountains of interior Mexico, to arduous climbs on peaks in Southern California, and to ancient cities which had never before been discovered. Each and every one of these situations had confronted me with my weaknesses, and my inability to grasp the fullness of my own vulnerability. Only much later did I ever have time to pause and reflect. I was going far too fast, speeding through my personal voyage without slowing down until I came crashing through realms of consciousness which forced me to touch the beyond, bringing my voyage back to the present. The present. I could feel the speed of the train, the racing of my heart, the pressure in my ears, and the extreme fear that there might not be another present moment if I didn't slow down and relish my current experiences. This very moment had to be a desperate desire to continue life. Would I live to relate the secrets of this private storm?

Just like in the movies, my life again began to flash before my eyes. I didn't care if anyone believed me or not. I had to live! I had to tell this story.

PROPHESY

The gentle eyes of knowingness,
  have followed me before,
    through time and space.
The eloquence still remains a memory.
But where and when eludes me still.
Then through the night like thunder,
  the pictures came,
    your tears, the rain . . .
      your soul, the wind . . .
        the moon, the stars, were at your command . . .
I need not ask why you've returned.
For the knowingness of your eyes,
  still commands me to go forth and be all that I can be.
So let us begin again,
  to create the world from which we came,
    to know that we are able . . .
The hurt is gone. All fear aside.
The condor reduced to ashes.
The mountain peaks and stars beyond,
  are ours.
    We are.
      We shall be . . .

— *Two* —

It was 1981. Hollywood was bustling with companies that needed catering during the filming of their commercials. That was my business, and I was doing quite well. So well, in fact, that I was catering for many stars in their homes. I was working long hours and had a real workaholic syndrome going. Even then, it wasn't enough to do all I was doing. I had a dream of opening a restaurant as well, and that dream manifested a couple of years later.

I had been psychically gifted since I was a small child, and had experienced many things in my 32 years. It was in this 32nd year of my life that the "gift," which I had so neatly tucked away in a long-forgotten closet, began to resurface with unbelievable forces of its own.

I had a home in Palm Springs, California, which I used as a get- away from my crazy schedule whenever I could. It gave me pleasure to escape the city and drive to the desert, where nobody could squeeze another ounce of time from me. Each time I went to this desert retreat, I recognized a presence in the house. I didn't know what else to call it, because it was too real to be my imagination. On the occasions when I had guests with me, they sensed it too.

On one occasion, three separate people woke up in the middle of the night, around three a.m., and felt some kind of energy coming from the southeast corner of the backyard. We all felt drawn to stare at that corner, not knowing why, and sensed a presence there. At first we believed that the house could have been built on top of an Indian burial ground, but upon checking with the local Tribal Council we found we were wrong. I returned later in the year, alone, and was astounded to see billions of tiny white lights floating in the air. They seemed to emanate from the sand in which I was lying in that section of the yard.

On another weekend, when I had three guests, one of the women said to me, "Jamie, I don't want to sound strange, but something woke me up last night and I was drawn to the window to look at your backyard. What's out there in the corner?" I was surprised at her comment, because I had never mentioned anything about it. The yard had not been landscaped; it was only sand.

None of the people who made such comments was psychic. An attorney and his wife who rented the house for a weekend told me that they were very curious about the house, because they experienced hearing voices during the night, much like overhearing murmurs. I even asked one of my guests if they thought it was the north wind, which sometimes rattled the windows in the house. But it had been a rare winter night and there had been no wind. Everyone agreed that the words were nearly audible and contained inflections that could not have been the wind. It was as if the voices came from someone who was very weak, and who was trying to reach across a vast expanse of time and space without enough voltage to span the distance.

Every person receives psychic information in a different way. I had been meditating and had experienced visions indicating that I was one of the people connected to the voices. Being a sensitive is no accident. Each soul carries that ability from lifetime to lifetime, making it easier to connect with others that are open to his or her gift. I felt it was no accident that I had bought this house with a friend, or that the voices were trying to get my attention, even through my house guests. It was more than just an eerie feeling of having something strange in the back yard. It felt as if someone was calling to me because they knew me. It brought up great emotional pain for me. I did not understand why it did so at the time, but grief welled up in me every time I sat alone in the yard looking at the far corner. When I put my hands in the sand and dug a foot or so down, the emotion was even stronger inside my chest. I got a lump in my throat and a heartache. The feeling was one of great loss. I knew that I had to look into this further, because it wasn't natural. I had no reason for feeling this way.

One weekend, upon returning to Hollywood, I called a fine British clairvoyant. From the information I had received, and from his perceptions, we pieced together the fact that there was some sort of energy-producing unit buried in the yard that was from a source far advanced to ours: a capsule of some kind. We went down to the house, located the exact spot, and decided to dig a hole and make some tests. When we dangled metal objects from a string over the spot, whatever was buried there pulled them from their normal position.

Later the next year, we had a team of experts from the Mutual UFO Network (MUFON) come with their instruments. This "network" was comprised of a group of writers, scientists, and investigators who had joined together to prove the existence of UFOs. Among other devices, they brought an ohmmeter, a tape recorder, and a microphone to perform various sonic measurements and energy experiments. Surges of energy registered on the machines when they were placed about five feet down in the hole. The instruments were also placed into a side hole which was dug two feet into the first hole's wall of sand and rock, and which was covered with about four feet of sand. Unfortunately, because of the existence of a power line twenty feet above the property and twelve feet behind the hole, the researchers did not choose to make any final conclusions. None of us had the money or the inclination to bring in a backhoe and dig fifty feet into the sand, which would have destroyed the yard and the neighbors' fences in the process. That would have been a major mining project and would have created a lot of curiosity. I had been proceeding on what I felt, while the MUFON team had been proceeding on instruments which had no feelings. It had been a marriage of opposites that frustrated both sides. The hole was subsequently covered without further exploration. I was not a quitter, and even though the frustration was great, I continued to seek for answers. The opinions of machines and of those who could not feel the energy were only a momentary setback for me. This didn't keep me from knowing what I had experienced. I knew there was a reason for it. The capsule had to be there for a reason, and I was determined to find out why.

The British psychic had told me to watch for certain con-stellations, and to look for where and when certain stars pointed towards the face of one of the mountains. He told me that there would be an ethereal light or reflection from the moon that would shine on an unusual kind of surface. I would find the spot. I was to meditate upon the mountain and observe a vision as it appeared. His instructions were very specific and accurate. He had also received impressions of a spacecraft in the hidden portion of the mountain—impressions which matched my own.

I took the entire following week off and journeyed to the desert. How strangely unlike me! Oh well, the results were well worth my "sacrifice." I prepared myself for the spring equinox, when the constellations would be in the proper posi-tion, and began my meditation.

After watching the stars and thinking I had found the proper place, I rose at dawn to traverse some of the foothills and pursue any further clues. I never realized how much rocks could look alike! The bruises and cuts from my first en-counter with the mountain began to ache. After five hours, I returned home. A hot bath and a nap were in order.

After my nap, I made a quick sandwich and started to work. It would be dark soon, and I wanted to see the moun-tain at sundown before I began my meditation. I sat facing the mountain, noticing for the first time that the entire mountain was a reddish-brown. To my left, high above a telephone pole which had earlier blocked my view, was a section which was truly different. Even its color was very curious. That had to be it. I ran inside to get my binoculars so I could scan it once more. Yes, that had to be the place. Nobody would have noticed it on so large a mountain—unless, of course, they had been looking for it as specifically as I had been.

I recalled the British psychic's words: "You will notice that a portion of the mountain is different. It will seem to emit a kind of ethereal light." I raced to my notes to see if I had remembered correctly. Yes, it was there! I ran to the front porch and saw how the angle of the Big Dipper led me to that exact point. It had to be correct.

As night blanketed the desert, I watched the crimson sky fade to lilac and finally to indigo. The warm glow inside me spoke of a sense of adventure and a feeling of inadequacy at the same time. I reflected on what it would mean if a spaceship were found intact. I had had a vision, from some other life, that somewhere in that valley, nine energy-producing devices had been left by spaceships. I had heard rumors that our world's governments had killed people for discoveries like these, that would upset what we were "supposed" to know. I was a bit fearful, but I also sensed a sort of protection that would keep me from harm's way. My thoughts began to drift into what it would be like to help humanity realize its true past. Did we once fly over our planet? If so, how do we explain our present state of affairs? How could we be so conceited as to believe we were isolated from the rest of God's creation? Why in the world would this tiny blue orb be the only place in the universe to have intelligent life? Worse still, how could we be so pompous as to limit the power of omnipotent creation? I could feel life in all things—the wind, the night sky—it all breathed the breath of life.

I walked outside again to scrutinize the mountain. The canyon wall was blackest black. Even the spot I had found with the binoculars was bathed in darkness. It was hard to discern the lines of my secret canyon. The moon had traveled far behind the mountain top, and starlight was the only light available. I was cold and windburned. The sinking feeling in my stomach returned.

What if I failed? Was the vision I experienced in Los Angeles just my imagination? I knew that, for some reason, I was connected to that spaceship. I had remembered a lifetime from long ago that bespoke a great disaster. I had remembered ships flying above me. It hadn't been a dream. I had been awake! Surely there was some reason for the vision. I was too hard-working to waste time on anything that wasn't of vital importance. I felt silly. Why was I questioning what I knew had to be the truth? Even as a child, I told my mother that she was not my mother. I told her that my home was on the planet of Uva. She dragged me to the psychologist at age four, only to be told that I was bright and well-adjusted. Why was I remembering childhood visions now?

I became determined. I had always fought for what I saw and what I knew. I had been ridiculed all my life and was not going to take it anymore. If this was a test of my belief in myself, I was going to find out, one way or the other. I didn't mind being wrong—I just wanted to know the truth.

I looked to the mountain. It was still occluded. I had decided to go back into the house when suddenly a light caught my eye. I looked to the sky and saw the light, moving east to west. It was like a satellite, or so I thought. I focused more intensely, and saw that it was actually composed of five lights that were green, red, and white. "Must be a really fast plane," I thought. Then the object surprised me. It darted rapidly in a zig-zag pattern and disappeared behind the mountain. It had to be them—whoever "they" were!

I was tired of doubting myself and listening to the opinions of those who were not like me. I giggled as I thought of the addictions they had to their left brains, and how this form of thinking controlled them through their own fears. Fears that they might be subjected to the harrassment of their peers. I was no fool — I knew that planes had red, green, and white lights. My father was a pilot, and I had been around planes since I was thirteen. This was no plane. Planes don't fly vertically and then zig-zag. Still lost in the thought of how right I was, I forgot the mountain!

Had I not been so caught up in my own musings, maybe I would have been paying closer attention. I wheeled around and looked at the mountain. There it was — the light that I had been told would lead my way. It was a V-shaped light coming from the canyon, about 3,000 feet up, and emanating from further up the canyon walls. Relief flooded every portion of my being. I had passed the test so far. Tomorrow I would go to the bottom of that area and find out how to reach the spot.

Morning came early, as I had spent the night in fitful sleep. I had been fighting myself for the right to change my own future if events brought cause to do so. My little beagle, Star, was eager to begin the day, but all I could do was let her out to run. Even the coffee seemed flat. What was happening to me? Here I was, embarking on a wonderful adventure, and all I could think of was how out of shape I was and that I was going to have a real tough time climbing that far. What if I fell? How would anyone know I was there?

I put on my hiking shoes and grabbed my parka, camera, binoculars, canteen, and Star. I packed the car and was off. Searching for a way to get to the bottom, I kept checking the map I had bought from the ski and pack shop. Finally, I found the way and arrived at the base.

I never could have imagined how big that mountain was. I would have to hike eight miles before reaching the place where the canyon began to rise. I had long ago learned what it meant to be a spiritual warrioress: with every ounce of energy, and with every portion of one's being, to seek the answers to the "Sacred Mystery." Within the framework of my personal quest, I had studied Native American medicine in Mexico and Texas. The rocks I would be climbing over were as big as my car, even on the flats. As a spiritual warrioress, I knew better than to indulge myself, but this seemed impossible.

The psychic from England had been very specific in his vision and instructions to me. "Look for a shelf-like rock. . . it's more than a ledge. . . it will be surrounded with other rocks of a brown-pink color but it will be different. You must get to the top by noon, for at midday there will be a shadow that will fall on a cross or X-like mark in the rock. That will be the point of entry; it shouldn't take much digging to get in."

I scanned the canyons and there was my target, high on the mountain. Yes, this was it. Me and the mountain. Oh brother, this was going to take a miracle — even more of a miracle if I could get past the no-trespassing signs. I was determined, but not stupid! I went home to sort it out.

After several calls to the local authorities and to Riverside, I made a trip to the tribal council offices. Nobody knew whose land it was. I finally located the person in charge and got the permission. I would have to cross a section of land owned by the state, another owned by Native Americans, and then county land. It was all set. My final call was to my own company for help. One of my friends, who was working for me at the time, agreed to drive down and accompany me the next day. Rick arrived late that evening, looking exhausted. We decided to go to dinner, and I filled him in on the situation.

"Rick, you're not going to believe this, but I've had a real mystical experience. The other night when I was meditating, I felt a force of some kind pull me out of my body, and I ended up on that mountain," I said. "I don't really know how to describe it to you. I was just meditating, trying to calm myself and clear the thoughts in my head, when I started feeling sick to my stomach. I got very light-headed and then glided into a calmer feeling as I set aside my fear of what was happening. I began to see pictures, but they appeared at first through a sort of fog. As I concentrated, they became clearer. It was as if a power was flowing through me that connected me with millions of tiny strings to my body and to the top of the mountain at the same time."

"Oh, I'd believe it," he replied. "You were really getting into some amazing stuff there a few weeks ago. Remember when you had that happen at the house during the football game? You were sick to your stomach and had to go outside and lie on my driveway just to get it to stop. I looked at your face and you were white as a sheet."

I did remember. "I was scared to death! I hate it when I can't control the way that happens. It's like going down a roller coaster with no bottom, only to discover that you're actually going up," I continued. "I've heard that it's called psychic sickness. Energy literally flows through your body, and you feel out of control. If you resist it, you end up with nausea or a headache. Thank God it was different this time."

The waiter arrived to take our order, and I waited to tell the story of my experience. "I got a little sick this time, but it eased up when I did some deep breathing. It felt like I was in a time warp, and that I was going far, far back into time. It's like you know you're in 1984 and are seeing right in front of you, in 1984, another vision of the past or future. In this vision, I was bathing in a pool carved by a mountain stream. It was exactly like a shallow bathtub — just right for one person. I got out and was sunning myself dry by the waterfall, when I saw a man yelling and waving to me at about a forty-five degree angle from my left. His eyes were brown and his hair was dark, full-collar length, and parted on the right. He wore a white, Nehru-style jacket. On its left side sparkled a silver emblem over the heart; the emblem was shield-shaped, and flashed prisms in its center. There seemed to be stairs up to where he was that were soft, like swirls of living rock cascading down to the bathing pool. He called me Luya. I got on a toga-like dress and ran to meet him."

Rick asked how I had known it was me. "I was in that body, using her eyes," I replied. "I could see only what she saw from that angle, and no more. It wasn't as if I was a fly on a rock. I was there, inside her. You see what I mean?" I asked.

"Sure. It's like knowing that you are you," he mused.

"That's right. It just felt too real," I said.

As we ate, I couldn't wait to tell him the rest of my story. "Rick, I may be going crazy, but I'm a happy lunatic if I am," I laughed. "This is really strange, because I don't remember how we went into our home, but that mountain is hollow. I was inside there. We had a two-seater scout ship. It was teardrop-shaped, with a pointed front and a round back, and made of a dark silver metal. On top was a clear bubble about eight and a half feet long by five feet wide. I remembered that its steering mechanism was in the pilot's helmet, attached by suction to his right temple — the intuitive side of his brain. His thoughts were projected by what was called a protein computer, and the ship flew on his thoughts alone. When anyone on any frequency in the universe wanted to communicate with him, there was a round quartz crystal that projected six-inch, pale chartreuse holograms into the cockpit. The pilot spoke telepathically, and the computer in his helmet projected his hologram to whoever he wanted to reach. A real UFO." I waited for this to sink in, watching Rick's face.

He sat there, steady as they come. Reliable Rick. Not a beat was dropped as he exclaimed, "Great, let's go get it!" I couldn't believe my ears. No shock, no surprise. Considering his background, I was taken aback. Rick had studied film-making in college, and then became a stockbroker. Now that's stable in my book! The corporate world was never my cup of tea, and it turned out not to be for Rick either. He had returned to his first love, which was directing films, but was helping me keep my company going in the mean time.

Noticing my attitude of quiet observance, Rick said, "Jamie, when I was in school, I was a science-fiction buff. I knew that the real way to the future was to apply the stuff that fiction is made of. You know I believe in reincarnation. You know I believe in creativity. Just where do you think creative guys get all their information? You don't really think it's just out of the blue, do you?"

Happy and relieved, I continued my story, commenting that the pictures in my vision had been disjointed. "The next thing I saw was a room, living quarters. The bed was made of a very large round, flat rock covered with furs and some sort of cushion. The man, my husband, was leaning over me. My head was bandaged. I had fallen," I explained. "I don't know how it happened, because the next picture I saw was a horrible war of some kind. Saucers in the sky."

I continued that there had been some sort of call over a communications system, and that my husband had rushed off. "He made me promise to keep the cavern and its contents safe, and I promised not to go outside. I knew that I would never see him again. The last thing I saw was the ship exiting through solid rock, as though it were an illusion. I must have died there. That's all I remember."

We finished dinner. Rick was lost in thought. Finally, he looked at me and said, "I imagine that the promise has been activated in your memory because you've just come into contact with the physical area again. That would explain the funny goings-on at the house." I felt so safe. I knew that here was someone who would understand. I would be okay, and the trip to the top of the canyon would be all right. On the way home, I pondered the possibilities the morning would bring, and was happy about the prospects.

Morning! I nodded myself into a vaguely coherent state. Knocking on Rick's door, I was rewarded with a muffled grumble. Coffee to the rescue! After we were both fully conscious, we loaded the backpack and headed to a diner for eggs. I was on pins and needles. With breakfast out of the way, we were off to the mountain.

I was really glad that we had left Star, my beagle, at home. The hike was grueling. Rick was in great shape, but I lagged behind like a wounded deer. The first stretch wasn't too bad, even though we had to scale canyon walls and then go into a valley to gain only a half-mile as the crow flies. During several stops, we were forced to decide which way to hike just to avoid dead-ends. Finally, we finished crossng the eight-mile flats. It seemed as though the ledge we needed to reach was forever in front of us. I was beginning to wish for a yellow brick road, no matter how far it was to Oz!

A few miles behind us, we had noticed a stream bubbling out of nowhere. Its snow-fed waters were delicious. Now that we were at the bottom of the real climb, I could see that the waterfall cascading from the top of the ledge was identical to the one in my vision. I followed it up the face of the rock, and pointed out where I had seen the ship fly through the stone embankment. It was just as I had seen. I was anxious to reach the top.

I flashed on my bandaged head in the vision. This was it. I had fallen here before. Suddenly I retched, and cowardice gripped me. When it finally dissipated, Rick was already across rock and standing on the ledge. I sat down and cried, exhausted and terrified. Rick kept talking to me, and he scrambled back across the gap. Mustering my courage, I began climbing down. I had to hang by my hands over the edge and drop to a five-inch-wide shelf in the rock. If I missed, I was dead. Rick caught one of my feet and placed it on the shelf; the other one slipped from the gravel. He grabbed me. I was facing the rock, hearing only my heart in my ears. When I became calmer, Rick jumped across the gap and reached for my hand. I was on the ledge. I was safe, though still reeling from the jump.

I was three feet from a sheer drop, on firm ground, but I still had to traverse 30 feet to get off the ledge and into an upper canyon. I scurried across and rounded the corner.

The hidden valley above us was heaven itself. We had seen wildflowers all the way up, but this particular setting was unbelievably lovely. I looked to the stream fifteen feet below me — there was the pool! Screaming with joy, I ran to it, pulling off my sweatshirt and shoes. My leotard was soaked with perspiration and I was ready for a dip. I pulled off my jeans and put my feet into the water. What a shock! I was overheated, but the water was like ice. So much for the dip. I settled for wiping my head and arms with a wet bandanna, and admired the multicolored wildflowers growing in profusion on both sides of the bubbling stream. Green grass and Irish moss covered the banks.

As I washed my face, I noticed the view for the first time. The canyons on both sides formed a "v" down to the desert floor. "There used to be lush green jungle down there," I said. "I remember seeing this in the vision when I was bathing here. It was truly beautiful at one time, Rick. Do you think we could have been so stupid as to destroy Eden?" I was asking myself, really. We both knew the answer. Our planet was hellbent on doing it again, if it had the opportunity. We ate our fruit and cheese in silence, watching a red-tailed hawk circle and lizards run by. It all seemed so beautiful, so dreamlike. My earlier fear of falling was worlds away.

I recalled the billions of white lights we had seen shining from the very ledge we were sitting on. We had first noticed them when we stopped to decide which canyon to scale. Rick had commented, "I've seen those lights before. I just always thought of them as an affinity flow from nature."

I understood what Rick was saying. It was what you would expect from a rock or plant sending you love in return for your admiration of all creation. There had to be some energy that nature put out. Physics teachers even said that energy could not be destroyed, just changed. The plants here certainly got enough of the sun's energy!

Finishing lunch, I suddenly flashed on my vision again. It felt as if someone were trying to turn my head so I would look behind me. I scurried upstream about fifteen feet, and there was my stairway! It was fabulous. Limestone rock, gently carved out like a set of stairs, serpentine, as if someone had melted the rock for just that purpose.

Again the time-warp effect came over me. I sensed that I was there, in that other time. I saw a man's back before me. He was lasering the rock with a gun of some sort. As I was drawn up the stairs to the upper level above the pool, I began to feel very weird.

At the top were three monolithic, reddish-brown rocks, three times my own height. I was drawn to the face of the one facing the valley below. The man gestured with his gun, directing me to look up to the top of one. I yelled at Rick to come. "Oh my God," he said. "Your Englishman was right. We never would have seen this 'X' if we hadn't been here at midday."

"Look at it, Rick, the sun's own shadow makes it very clear!" I exclaimed. The man smiled and walked away behind the monoliths. I ran to follow, but he was gone. I searched to find the place he could have disappeared to, and tried to find an opening in the giant rock. The only opening was too small for an adult to get through. Looking more closely, I saw that the opening was covered with pink granite that looked as if it had been melted. It was decomposed, like hardened sand. I called to Rick and he agreed with me. This must be the place to dig. The entrance to the cavern below had to be here.

Rick retrieved a small, short-handled pick from his pack. Returning, he said, "Hey, Jamie, what's that mark on the rock behind you? It looks like a carved drawing of an animal." I looked. Just about a foot from my hand was indeed a drawing, resembling a lizard. The figure was walking, as a lizard would, hanging on the rock sideways and paying no attention to gravity.

We had found a lizard buried in the sand when we had dug the hole in the backyard at the house. It hadn't run away, but had stayed curled in my hand for an hour. Was there a connection?

I was quite sunburned, having shed my parka as the temperature rose. I wanted shade. Rick agreed to have first go at the opening, so I went a few feet down the slope to sit behind a big grey rock. With the first blow of the pick, thousands of echoes sounded. I could see Rick's bronzed muscles ripple and go slack. "Hey, look at this!" he yelled. "There are lots of lizards coming out to watch."

I sauntered up the slope and saw at least fifteen lizards, all different colors. I knew they weren't chameleons. I was amazed at the variety of colors: grey, white, beige with orange scales, green, and one the color of a peacock's feather. They were all just watching me. They didn't move, run, or show fear. I was delighted. I decided to try talking to one who sat two feet above the lizard carving, but the words wouldn't come and I was sure that Rick would think I was stupid.

Then I thought a minute, and decided to just talk to him telepathically. I knew some people could speak to animals this way, and there was no harm in trying it. In my mind, I said, "Hi, little lizard. If you know a way to help us dig into this entrance, please let me know."

Almost instantaneously, I heard a voice in my head speaking in a Cockney accent. "Yer at the wrong angle, mate. If yer want to get in, 'it 'er from above." I jumped back in shock. This must have scared the little guy, because he scurried into a hole and was gone.

Just how was I going to tell Rick that one? Oh boy, I really got what I asked for! I called to Rick, "You look kind of tired. You want me to give it a go?"

"It's okay, just a little while longer. I'll let you take your turn — don't worry," he answered. Oh well, I tried. I went back to my shady spot to wait.

Rick continued to plug away at the hole, which was getting larger, but still not nearly large enough. He kept on hitting smaller rocks, which sent shocks through his arms and shoulders. This whole situation was really making me nervous. I didn't know how much I could say without Rick thinking I was nutty.

I looked around the valley within this sheltered canyon, and then to the sky and back to the desert far below. I never twiddle my fingers. I was doing it, though, like playing a piano on the rock. Waiting was not fun. I looked at my right hand. What was that I heard? I began to knock on the rock. It echoed. Good Lord! The thing was hollow! For it to be sounding back like that, it had to be very thin. "Hey Rick, take a break. Come here," I yelled. "Listen to this! The thing is hollow!"

Rick dropped the pick and wiped his face as he answered, "It could be the loose sheets of rock on top, like back there on the ledge."

I looked again and listened. I didn't agree. "Rick, the echo is too hollow-sounding for it to be a sixteenth of an inch. The slate's flaking off. That's all there is where it's loose."

He was at my side, peering at the loose rock. "Maybe you're right," he said, knocking his fist against the canyon floor.

"Rest a while and I'll take my turn," I giggled. I grabbed the leather gloves and was off to see whether my friend, the lizard, was right. Rick had been stuck for about twenty minutes on one particularly tough spot. I climbed a couple of feet from where he had been and gave a mighty heave-ho. It was close but didn't hit the right spot. The second blow was the one. Three feet of granite came tumbling down.

I was laughing so hard, Rick had to look. "How did you do that!?" he yelled. I came down to tell him the story of the lizard. He was angry that I had let him work that hard, but was understanding about my talk with the little lizard. He had no qualms about that type of thing. He even had a story or two of his own.

We talked about the guardians of nature, and how animals were an extension of the spirit world who were there to guide us. It was through honoring these little brothers of the animal kingdom that we were allowed to experience the secrets of their sacred spaces. Only a few hours ago, a great scorpion with his majestic stinger had warned us away from another probable place to dig. I wasn't sure how much of my medicine teachings I could share with Rick. We had never talked much about this other world that I felt a part of. It was good to know that he had held back too. In sharing this experience, we bonded as friends on a new level that had no place in the tinseltown reality we had both chosen to endure in order to follow our separate dreams.

Then it was time to get back to work on the entrance. Rick decided to take over again and walked up the slope. I noticed the back of the upper canyon's far ridge. A cold breeze was blowing in, and as it hit my sunburn, I began to get the chills. A storm appeared to be brooding over the crest, and the sky suddenly filled with enormous thunderclouds.

There was no shelter and only two apples left. We would have to leave soon to get down the mountain safely. Tears sprang to my eyes, and I was filled with a sense of loss. "Damn it! Why, when we were so close, did it have to storm? I can't leave now. I'll never make it up that mountain again if we have to leave. Why? It's so unfair!" I thought. Rick had noticed the storm too, and started talking to me about leaving. I was still lost in thought.

As I was silently crying, I heard a Voice in my head. *"Not now, my child. Now is not the time. It will come. Be patient."* I asked the Voice if I were making a mistake. Was this not for me to find?

It answered, *No, little one, you are doing the right thing. The Earth's people are not yet ready for the secrets within this place. You have been led this far to teach you how to see and hear our words. You will return to use the secrets to aid your world. That is why you were returned to Earth."* Rick had packed up and was urging me to get going. It was raining. I had to stop my communication with the Voice and go. My heart was heavy on the way down, yet glad at the same time. I couldn't understand the duality of it, but I was touched by the love I had experienced.

The climb down was rugged, and my ankle was constantly getting into crevices that turned it enough the wrong way to make it feel like the muscles were being stretched. I was not really concentrating on where to put my feet, and the rocks were getting looser with the cooling rain. However, the colors of the mountains were coming alive as the rain bathed and brightened the musky rose hues. The fantastic fragrances of steamy earth mixed with early wildflowers and desert sage sent me back to my feelings of joy at hearing the Voice, and for the moment overrode my sinking feeling of having failed at some level to penetrate the rock and enter the mountain and my past.

As we finally reached the car and unloaded the backpack, the storm grew a bit more alive. Every muscle in my body was screaming for a massage and hot water. I didn't feel too cold, since I was overheated from the hike, but as I cooled down on the drive back to the house, my needs became a chapped and aching longing to hit the rack. We ate at home after hot baths and drank some hot chocolate before bed. Rick was in great spirits and planned to stay up and watch some movies. It was all I could do to say goodnight and drag myself to my bed.

That night I awoke suddenly, with pictures flashing in my mind of an all-out war which had taken place in that time long ago. The Voice was ringing in my ears and the explosions shook me to the very core of my being.

"Yes, little one, there was a terrible war here 15,000 years ago and you were witness to it. Your world will be ready for this information in the years to come. Seven cities were lost, and the myth of them is still recorded by the Native Americans, who are the remnant race of Lemuria, called Mu or the Motherland. The freedom fighters were a collective of many extraterrestrial civilizations that came here to start a new seed race to allow this planet to live in peace. The lost cities of Cibola are no myth. The word Cibola *means buffalo and is represented by Taurus. Your group was working with those from the Pleiades then. The Seven Sisters and the Seven Cities are connected here and in the constellation of Taurus."*

I had a million questions, but the Voice vanished and I was left alone with my feelings. The unrest in my soul was like a torrent of shattering, nerve-splitting sounds that brought colors and surges of energy to my solar plexus.

The deafening screams for help, mercy, deliverance, rang in my dream memory from voices gone for thousands of years. The smell of burning flesh and the gruesome colors of war were not from any war that I had ever consciously known, but from a war with laser bombs that melted anything in sight. A vague face from my dream said that the ultimate bombs had been used, composed of a sandwich of hydrogen and itrium that created the worst possible devastation. They created a collapse of atomic structure, a boiling of all elements together. Metal, rock, flesh, and plant life pooled into a mass of frothing sand. Dear God, this couldn't be real.

The voices from the capsule in the backyard were trying to warn me that it had happened before, when humanity's technical expertise had surpassed its connection to the Source and to nature. We had to wake up and learn to live in harmony or it would happen again.

The knot in my stomach and the pain in my heart kept me pondering on the waste of it all. I felt so small, so alone, so helpless. I could only pray and believe that others were doing the same, for it was too much for me to bear alone. The depth of what I had seen was crippling my senses and making me want to shut down my feelings, becoming a hermit inside myself. I sat in my solitary silence awaiting the promise of another azure desert dawn.

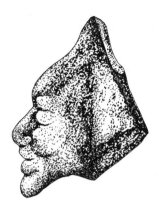

UNQUENCHABLE LOVE

If you took my heart out
    and burned it for an age,

It would be blackened and burned.

But you could never burn out
    the love planted there
        by the hand of one I have never known.

— *Three* —

F all, 1982. My emerald-green office, with its fourteen-foot ceilings, had walnut furniture that stood out against its green walls and white trim. A brass ceiling fan wafted a breeze towards me as I worked at my desk. I pondered my brass-framed collection of cigar box tops, realizing that I couldn't maintain my train of thought.

It had been three months since I had gone up the mountain, and I was back into a routine of twelve- to twenty-hour days. Each night when I had gone home I had meditated for hours, but there was no way I could recreate the same feeling. What or who was that Voice? The regular world seemed mundane by comparison. I had to finish my work and get back into the swing of life.

Something funny started happening in the pit of my stomach. I was nauseous and experienced a feeling of falling. "Here it comes again — I'm being pulled out of my body!" I thought as I fought the sensation. Gulping air and hanging onto the arms of my swivel chair, I tried to look around the room. The wall before me shimmered. It was as though a form were glittering in front of my eyes. I calmed myself, working to stabilize my pulse and breathing. There was a being before me, not a man, and yet not really a woman. The glowing shape was like ripples in a pond that went out only to the perimeters of the form.

"*Greetings little one, Daughter of Isis. Awaken unto yourself. The time has come for you to remember,*" the Voice said. I quickly grabbed a pen to jot down what she was saying. It was a woman. "*You have forgotten that your purpose here is to help your fellow man. You must find love in your heart for all of the creatures here. It is the law of love that will solve any dispute you have with your fellows,*" she continued.

"Who are you?" I asked. The Voice continued as if the

question had not been asked.

"The planet of Uva is the third planet from Betelgeuse in the constellation of Orion. Long ago that star system was invaded by beings from Ursa Major. The beings from Orion were losing their connection to God and were easily influenced by the promises of power from the invaders. A handful of the children of nobles and rulers in Orion refused to buckle to the control and began to fight that darkness. Their emblem was the Black Dragon. The dragon was the symbol for God, the all-knowing force that could fly through the darkness unheeded and breath fire and light into the cosmos."

I quickly asked, "Is that why Palm Springs is now a desert? Did we fight there?"

"Yes, and you lost because you fought with nuclear laser bombs that destroyed millions of atoms that were universes yet unborn. The dark beings of Orion had infiltrated Atlantis and it was the period of the third fall. They could not help you. Nor could the beings from the Seven Cities, nor could Ra from Venus. Everyone lost because they had forgotten that war solves nothing. It was after this time that interstellar commerce ceased on Earth."

"Why were we here on Earth? The Black League, I mean."

"Little one, you were offered a place to rest and recuperate and had many hollow mountains in which to hide. Many are still operating stations for the Galactic Confederation today. All of you are here to learn again the ways of peace and to serve your fellow man as emissaries of the light, for you have lost the memories that you must regain. You will learn from lives you have had before and can then make the connection to the Creator an invincible one."

I was startled, yet it felt right. I knew I had been sent here for something. I asked, "Then all those childhood dreams were merely flashbacks of other lives?"

The Voice replied, *"You are one of millions of wandering souls that are of the starseed race, returned to Earth to aid the transition of this world into Eden once again. You are precious to us. Now is the time. Remember these words and you will know what to do. We will guide your steps to find joy in your life. Do not be afraid. You are protected. The choice is yours now. We will be watching."* The Voice faded, along with the glimmer on the wall.

I was crying, tears slowly etching their way down my chin. I had never felt that I belonged here on Earth, but I had always tried to work hard, to be a success so that my life would help the world. That was my attempt at winning a place in life. Touched by the love I felt in my heart, I longed to hear those words again. I had been right. There was a reason why I had been different. All those years of seeing what others could not see, and hearing what they could not hear, were for a reason. All the verbal abuse from my growing years didn't matter anymore. I had run from my gift. I had tried to be like the other kids in school, but they had been frightened when I told them what I thought based on my "third sight." Now all those years and the hurt I had felt were being replaced by love. It was okay. Every misunderstanding, every session of name-calling every night of wanting to be at their parties, seemed like a bad dream. That dream was now replaced by love.

In college, I had thrown myself into my artwork and had developed many friendships, but I had never mentioned my gift. Now, I would be able to find some way to truly help others. I didn't have to curse my gift anymore — it was there for a reason. I had waited 32 years to find this out, and my tears were joyful.

My thoughts turned to Molly, a girl I had known in Austin, Texas who had had a rough life. As an abandoned child, Molly had been taken in by a madam at a Texarcana cathouse and taught the "trade" at the tender age of eleven. At sixteen she had gotten pregnant, and her baby had been sold to a childless couple. One day Molly finally ran away, and she wandered around making a living the only way she knew how. When I met Molly years later, it was when she was getting married. I observed something special about Molly. She had a heart of gold, and was always helping people look to the bright side of life. Her walnut, tousled hair curled into coal-black eyes when she laughed. She would always joke that her wild, black Irish hair was the only attribute she had left. I disagreed. Her skin was whitest porcelain, and even though her face had been ravaged by a hard life, she lit up when she smiled. Molly had been a wonderful friend to many, and I was no exception.

Molly and Clarke, her husband, had come to visit while I was out one night. I never kept the door locked during those days. They had waited for me, watching TV, and then finally left. I returned late from a concert and found their note on my sketch pad. I laughed at how they put their thank-you: "We ate some sandwiches, drank your last beer, watched the tube, and we thank you very much!"

Weeks later, looking through my sketch book, I found Molly's other note:

> *Dear Jamie,*
>
> I'm gonna ask you a favor because I know you will understand. I won't be around much longer. I feel it coming from down inside my bones. You are strong, much stronger than my Clarke, please take care of him.
>
> One day you will tell the story of your gift, and it will set free all those grief-stricken folks who can't talk about how they feel inside. You won't always be driftin' through your private storm. The time will come for you to give some answers to others.
>
> Love,
> *Sweet Molly Malone*

Three-and-a-half weeks later, the small sports car which Molly, Clarke, and a friend were riding in ran under a gasoline truck. The boys lived, but our Molly was gone. I had known Molly for only three months, but a bond had formed between us that would last forever.

A new tear now trickled down my cheek, and I sent Molly my love. She had known. She was right. I knew I would find my way.

STARCHILD ECSTASY

I have tasted of the nectar
     that was not meant for man,
          and borne the pain of too much love
           the best that I can.

But I was never of this world
     though here I must remain
          to try and match the foolishness
           of all these earthly games. . .

— *Four* —

It seemed as if April and May had slipped through my fingers. I had been working very hard. Spring rains had washed Los Angeles, June was on her way, and I was thrilled with the thought of a break from work during the hiatus for the film companies.

One afternoon, I left the office early to visit a friend in Pasadena. Twenty or so people were going to have dinner and then attend a meeting. I was deeply concerned about my business. The restaurant had been open for nine months, but the catering company was still paying all the bills for both businesses. The pressure was enormous, and I was really scared. I was responsible for the paychecks of 23 people and the families they fed. The restaurant was just squeaking by, and the equipment loans were coming due.

I wandered out to the pool to sit quietly and think. The backyard was empty, so I picked a chaise lounge and just tried to relax. My mind wandered, trying to find some solutions. The business was really touch-and-go. Would I lose all I had worked for these hard and fast years? How could I let down the people who had helped me? The implications were staggering.

Each of the faces of those who had believed in my talent and ability flashed before me, and I began to cry. I was angry and hurt. Failure was not in my plans. I wanted to make it all okay, but I felt so helpless. I looked to the sky as it enveloped me with its warm, late-afternoon light, and began to think of my shimmering spirit friend. Mentally, I called out to her, hoping my call would be heard. "Why am I feeling this pain? My heart is broken! So many people count on me. I have to make it. Please help me find a miracle!"

There was no answer. I walked around the garden, but was in no mood to keep my mind off business. Even the geraniums were bland in comparison to the fire which consumed my reasoning powers. It was stupid to be angry — I would just have to find a way. There was always an answer — always.

I returned to my chaise and looked at the sky. There they were! The little white lights. Everywhere! Excited, I ran to the house and called my friend Avery. "Avery, quick, come here. Don't tell anyone else, just come here." My friend, Lila, followed. "What are you two up to?" she asked.

"Oh Lila, you've known me forever it seems. You'll understand. I don't want to influence either of you, so just look at the sky and tell me what you see." Both ladies had children my age, and I felt like a fool asking them to look at the sky. If they didn't see the lights, I would really feel stupid.

"Why, there are lots of little white lights, swarming like mosquitoes," Lila said.

"Oh yes, I see them," Avery said. "I've seen them a lot before. I always thought it was some sort of reflection from the back of the retina due to the sun. The sun is nowhere above us, so it must be a flow of some kind."

"I've told both of you about my experience in Palm Springs. Lila, you were there with me one weekend. Remember those lights in the backyard?"

"Sure," she said, "they were coming from that hole you dug. How could I forget that? I really felt strange."

"Well, I just wanted to make sure that someone else saw them," I replied as Avery started into the house. "Yeah, they're real all right," she said, rounding the patio door.

Lila lingered a moment, looking at me. "Jamie Sue, you amaze me sometimes. You're really special. I think you'd notice a pine needle if it fell in the middle of a forest."

I turned red at the compliment. I had never been able to accept compliments graciously. "Thank you," I mumbled. "I'm just going to go back and rest for a little while."

Lila returned to the house, and I went to the chaise to think. Every time I had seen the lights, some kind of energy had been present. I was staring at the sky, trying to figure it out. The sun was behind the tall cypresses at my back, and the pool reflected their shadows in its watery way. I tried to find the common denominator. The lights, the desert, the mountains, the city: it just didn't gibe that way.

The sky was filled with small, puff-like cumulonimbus clouds, gently moving east. What was that? I saw a brief change in one of the clouds overhead, and began watching it closely. I couldn't believe it — it wasn't moving! Only the others moved. Thunderstruck, I was suddenly aware that something was behind that cloud. I mentally screamed, "Why are you hiding from me? I know you're there! I want to see you!" At the exact moment that these thoughts escaped my consciousness, a disc-shaped craft dropped abruptly from the bottom of the cloud and then rapidly returned to its original cloaked position. I couldn't even squeeze out the scream that had caught in my throat.

Words began forming in my head. The Voice said, *Do not worry, little one, all will be okay. Within seven days, your business will be all right. We promise you that your needs will be taken care of. Listen to our words, for you are to follow a difficult path. You will be different from this day forward. Your fingerprints have even been altered slightly. These will change the patterns of your life. You will be called upon . . . listen to your heart, for we will guide your steps."*

I couldn't move fast enough. I ran for Avery, and when Lila saw me wheel around the corner, she came on our heels. The three of us stood looking at the cloud. I had been able to spit out enough of an explanation for them to understand.

Lila spoke first. "Is that it? I think I see it." I pointed out the exact cloud and indicated how it was dipping out of the cloud mass at very short intervals. Yes, they saw it. Lila looked at me. I was hearing the Voice again.

"There will be a sign to you, little one, that will allow all of this to be recorded. It will be a manifestation of our love for you."

I was lost in time. After a few minutes, Lila touched my arm. "Jamie Sue, you should have seen your face. It was glowing. I couldn't hear the words, but I felt like you were being talked to." Lila's soft Texas drawl had wakened me from my dream-like state.

Avery said, "Well, you girls saw more than I did, but it was definitely something." Avery looked from my face to Lila's, then back to mine. "Well, it's for sure that something happened — the whites of your eyes are baby blue. Lila's eyes have just a cast to them, but yours are almost the color of that background blue on Delft pottery." I rushed into the house. The bathroom mirror was verification enough.

I immediately asked to use the phone and called Ann Druffel, an investigator for the Mutual UFO Network who I had met several months earlier. After I had relayed the series of events to her, she arranged for our stories to be documented. I returned to the pool to look for anything else, since Ann was interested in knowing if they were still there. The cloud had moved a bit, but others were still passing it by. Ann had written two books on UFO and parapsychological subjects and was a very objective investigator. She had done a study in 1983 on reported close encounters in southern California, which indicated that they had occurred upon so-called ley lines. These lines have been suspected by other researchers to constitute a sort of energy grid. The location of this house was on a ley line which Ann had quickly plotted since our last conversation.

I looked to the heavens once more, and heard the Voice speak. *"Your eyes will be blue for two days. This is a sign that you have been chosen for some important work. You will be sheltered in love. Be not afraid. There is hope and joy surrounding your efforts."* I had a thousand questions, but the cloud was gone — it just vanished before my eyes. My questions would have to wait.

Two days later, on Thursday, an article appeared in the *Los Angeles Times* food section about the top catering companies in town. My company was included. Calls and money began to roll in. The bills would get paid.

Sunday brought a further surprise. There, in the newspaper's Calendar section, was an article on my restaurant by Lois Duan. A rave review! I couldn't believe it, though I knew she had been in months ago. Now the phone was ringing off the wall for reservations, and I was lost in the wonder of it all. I would never forget just how all of this had occurred. I spoke a silent prayer of thanks to my sky brothers.

I felt that I had experienced a real miracle, and I knew that I would never again be the same. How had I gotten caught up in this world of "learning to forget?" I felt as if the child in me had come to life once again. I found the love and compassion that had somehow gotten lost in the world of money and careers. My soul began to sing of my vision quest, and of a poem I had written long ago.

VISION QUEST

I, being like most other fragile human beings
    have fantasies, upon which I
        Build my dreams.

On this musky summer's night,
    with the jutting branches above me
        carving crevices in the midnight sky,
            my fantasies have come to life.

Yet to touch them would be impossible,
    for they too shall face the topaz morning
        in their purity and innocence,
            and fade before my eyes.

There was a time when I was younger
    that dreams were very real
        and innocence a part of living.
I believed that the colors of the morning
    were born in my soul,
        and that place, being a safe harbor,
            would let me grow and flourish
                before my ever-watchful eyes.

True wonder of life still dwells within me,
    Undaunted by where I have been,
        and hopefully unchanged by where I am going.
God help me the day this magic dies.

I scanned the halls of my mind for the door that had brought me to my 22nd year of life, and began to reconnect with the test of my courage that had made me into a medicine woman.

It had been my first vision quest, and it was as fresh in my memory as when I had experienced it. I had chosen a location that had always brought me peace. The medicine man who was my teacher had staked me out in the canyon near a stream with a waterfall. I was living in San Luis Potosí, Mexico, singing with a Mexican band, and had begun my studies with this man, Joaquin a few months earlier. Now it was time to test the power of my connection to the Great Spirit.

There would be three days without water or food; three days of silent praying and purification. I trusted that the Great Spirit would give me the gift of vision so that I would see my pathway clearly.

I was allowed to see the water but not to touch or drink it, and the ensuing struggle was intense. After three grueling days of deprivation and intense prayer with no answers, I was ready to give up. The sun had baked me mercilessly and my lips were full of blisters. As the night came, I prayed harder than I ever had before to receive sustenance that would last me through until dawn.

Through many years of night skies, and of indigo dreams sprinkled with promises of wishes upon stars, the moon had always been my friend and silent companion. As she came up, I honored Grandmother Moon and allowed her to bathe me in her silver light, cooling the fire inside me and the scorched and agonized temple of my body.

She dressed herself in a crescent that night, with Venus, her companion in light, sitting beside her. Near midnight I prayed again and asked for some sort of sign, as I could no longer hold myself together. I knew that I was finally surrendering to the power of the Force, which was much greater than I was. I had opened to allowing the universe to live and flow through me.

At that moment, all the stars in the sky turned different colors before my eyes. I saw a canopy of jewels shining the colors of the universe down on me. The moon was surrounded by an electric indigo-blue heart, and the stars began to sing a song that I had never heard before. It was my power song, and was in a language I was not familiar with. I have since found out that it was Seneca, one of the tongues of the Iroquois.

I became a chalice and was filled with the wonders of the universe. My connection to the Great Spirit, and all of my relations with other living creatures, was reinstilled. When I came off the mountain, I knew that my Indian name was "Midnight Song." I knew also that I had come from the stars and that one day, when my Earth walk was finished, to the stars I would return.

That was my secret. I had become myself in the Native American way, on a vision quest in my own personal "power spot." With no food or water, I had communed with nature to purify my body, mind, and soul. This had allowed me to offer myself to the universe and to receive a vision of my purpose in this life. How long had it been since I had forgotten my self — my true self? I vowed that it would never happen again.

I began to review the steps of my personal history that had kept me from my true destiny, the destiny of being who I truly was — at all times. In my mind's eye, ten years of my life rolled before me as if I were reviewing a movie with the speed of quicksilver. There had been a lot of fear about being "different," and always there had been the mental pictures that told me what was about to happen. The faucet had been turned on full tilt without a cutoff valve.

It had been horrifying to be sitting next to someone I didn't know and see the pictures of what they were thinking, or to go to the grocery store and see the photos of missing children and know they were dead. I had worked with the police on two such cases and found that I became so involved in the mental images of what had happened that I couldn't sleep. I would have nightmares in which the children would be calling for help and screaming in anguish. When the children were found, they had been murdered, just as I had seen. I finally had to stop doing this kind of work. My gift seemed more like a curse, and I ran from it. I couldn't take it any more!

Then I learned how to control the mental pictures by cutting them off until I could choose to see them by remote viewing. I didn't go into the pictures anymore. I just pulled away from them as if they were a movie and I was the audience. Before I learned to remote view, I would have entered the body of the child in the picture and would have felt the pain, fear, and actual blows to the body that the child had suffered. In 1976 I had finally shut down totally, when the body of one of the children was found and bruises appeared on my body in the same places she had been bludgeoned.

From time to time when I wasn't watching myself, I would get pictures that belonged to someone else in the room I was in. Immediately I would throw up the psychic wall that I used to protect myself, and they would go away.

There were ten long years of trying to "be normal," when I threw myself into work so that I could prove to my family and to everyone else that I was able to function successfully in their world. The change finally came when I was told by a psychic in Los Angeles that I couldn't do what I was doing. That made me angry enough to open up again.

I had been invited to the home of Dr. Louise Ludwig, a Ph.D. in parapsychology, along with a group of other people. I had just opened the restaurant, and as this was the only day on which it was closed, I decided to attend the "circle." This is the name given to a gathering of people who come together in prayer and wish to do psychic work under the direction of spirit guides. I had never been to a Spiritualist circle, so it seemed like a fun idea, just to see what it was like.

In the center of the circle of people there were photos facing the floor and a drawing of some kind with a piece of white paper over it. During the two hours that I was there, I was amazed to find words getting stuck in my throat and the mental pictures coming to me as if I had never shut down. After most of the regular events, meditation, prayer, and sharing of psychic impressions of messages for various members, I finally broke into a laugh. The laugh was the result of an incredible amount of nervousness which finally crashed through the lump in my throat. Everyone looked at me totally horrified, and I quickly became beet red. I stammered, and then the words began to roll from my throat like a golden stream of liquid honeysuckle.

I began to tell everyone the story of the man whose picture and photos were under the paper on the floor. He was an Irish patriot who had lived hundreds of years before and had left a legacy to those who wanted peace in Ireland. I was astounded as I viewed the mental images coming to me and recounted intimate details of his life to the group. The woman who had placed his picture there sat wide-eyed and open-mouthed. She had been traveling to Ireland doing research on him for years, and had come by these same facts only after long and difficult investigation. She verified everything I had related, and suddenly I was very self-conscious.

After the meeting was completed, several people came up to me and thanked me for speaking up. The couple I had come to the circle with had a different opinion, however. The man was a professional psychic in his mid-fifties and was a bit upset with me. Apparently I had stolen the show and, unbeknownst to me, he was angry. In the following weeks he set out to make me believe that if I was to develop my gift I needed to be his student for six years. Finally, after a few months, he blew up one day after he had been drinking and told me that I was going too fast, and that my development had to be at his rate. Then he told several other people that I was not balanced, meaning he thought I was fantasizing and losing my grip on reality. That was the last straw — no one was going to tell me that I couldn't see what I saw or hear what I heard psychically. I had dealt with that issue extensively during my early years. I then began to meditate and do exercises that would enhance my will and power over the unseen world.

It had always been a fight, but in this moment in which I reviewed my past, recalling my vision quest, the power of who I was came to me. Just being myself and not wanting the approval of those I had considered my superiors was a big step forward. My new vision quest was beginning, and I had come light years since my first one. The lights of the night sky lit up in my heart and I felt myself growing stronger. My spirit soared and began to flee its earthly form, becoming one with the spirit of the night sky.

DREAMTIME

The pictures inside
   are real, it seems.
      They can leave you to ponder. . .

      Are you the dreamer?

      Or are you the dreamed?

— *Five* —

I spent much time alone in the late-night hours, rediscovering the way back to me. I listened for the Voice, but nothing came. I was learning patience in a very miserable way.

After a couple of weeks, during a meditation, she came. *"Find a mirror, my child. Look to your forehead and see the portion above your eyebrows."* I found a swivel travel mirror, placed it on a table, and arranged it at the proper angle. "What next?" I wondered.

The Voice said, *"Observe the obvious, be at one with it. Look to your body for the secrets to come."*

"But what do I do? This seems really stupid. What do you mean?" I cried out in confusion. The Voice was gone. I resigned myself to doing what I was told and just looked at the mirror. After fifteen minutes, I was really bored. Just as I was about to give up, a welt seemed to appear on my forehead. It was turning deep pink, and I rubbed it to see if it was real. It didn't hurt, but it was definitely there.

The cells in my skin seemed to be moving. They broke apart and took on the casts of different colors. Was I hallucinating? This was amazing! A form was appearing. I had started a journal after the sky brothers had come to me in Palm Springs, but the journal was in the living room, and I was afraid to leave the mirror and go get it. I opened the drawer and grabbed an envelope instead, keeping my eyes on the reflection in the glass.

A man, standing next to a pyramid, looked back at me from my forehead. His eyes were just smudges and he wore a fez. In his hand was a baton or scroll. I quickly sketched his figure and the pyramid, never once looking at the paper. My stomach convulsed in the fear that he would disappear. Just as I finished the line drawing, his image faded and another one formed. This one was the letter Z. A vertical line ran through the letter, forming a drop on the end. When this faded, an elephant's profile appeared, its ear pointed at the top. As soon as I had completed the elephant, a camel etched its way into the pink area that remained. Each of these images appeared over a three-inch-square area. It was astounding. I sat in awe as the last remains of the camel vanished.

My hair was down, and a natural center part had formed waves at the top of both sides of my forehead. A blue mist now covered those waves, and large, electric-blue eyes appeared just below them. The face that looked back at me covered all of my forehead and a portion of my hair. When I moved, it didn't. Those eyes were in the middle of a half-feline, half-human face. I had no real schooling in Egyptology, but this was an Egyptian cat goddess for sure! The face was in no way like the other figures. They had been inanimate figures; this face smiled and breathed. My hair seemed to move with every breath she took. I had long since stopped breathing myself and was suddenly scared. This image was floating free of my skin.

"Oh God, this is weird! I don't think I'm ready for this. I can't stop staring, though," I thought. I had to confront the image, like it or not. The eyes suddenly became gentle in a very comforting way and the fear vanished. Under the face, on my forehead, another symbol formed. As I looked at my skin below the face's mouth, the cat woman dissolved. She was replaced by an "ankh," the Egyptian symbol of life. The redness began to clear and I was left looking into the mirror, totally exhausted.

I wondered how I would ever be able to tell my friends what was happening to me. I decided I didn't even care. I would worry about that when it happened.

I began to live for my quiet time in the evenings. Life welled up inside of me like the July sun. One evening, after a grueling day over the restaurant ovens, I relaxed in the calm of the summer night. Alone in my living room, I lit a candle and began to meditate. The usual daylight-savings sounds of kids yelling and dogs barking were absent. The sun had long since taken his rest from the Hollywood sky, and the dark night was pregnant with a silence unusual for summer. Before I could even quiet my daytime thoughts, the Voice came.

"Go to Mexico. There are the secrets you seek. The city is buried deep beneath the soil. You will find the entrance to a sacrificial temple behind the third pyramid. You have been there before. Your memory will serve you well."

Pictures of Morelia flashed through my mind. Three years ago, when I had returned to the Villa Montana, I had seen two haystack-like objects high on a hill from my car window.

"When?" I asked.

"*When the new energy of the old year is complete. Near your personal new year,*" she replied.

"That would be October — my birthday," I thought. "Less than three months away." The Voice was gone.

I started preparations for the trip in my mind. This was truly an act of faith. If nothing else, it would be a well-deserved break.

A little shaken by the implications of it all, I called Linda, my closest friend for fifteen years. She had been following the events in my life and had provided invaluable support for me. Even though she was in Austin, she felt as if she were close by at all times.

"Linda, I want you to go to Mexico with me. I never got to pay you what I should have for flying out and helping me open the restaurant, so this is my gift."

After hearing all the details, she agreed without a second thought. "Jamie, I know that this will be a special time for both of us. We haven't actually been together for any length of time since my divorce. I know what it would mean to me. I'm even glad that it will be high up in the mountains so we won't be near too many tourists. I need some quiet time and some nurturing myself. I've been fighting to get back those parts of me that I lost. The last thing I need right now is the singles nightlife."

I was pleased. Linda attracts men everywhere she goes. Her sparkling green eyes and below-the-waist blonde hair seem to knock 'em dead every time. If they only knew how spiritually in tune she is, they would be truly astonished.

Linda is a dreamer. The psychic part of her makeup comes in dreams, and she is very accurate. She is fluid water energy of the highest order. Water energy is female earth energy: the ability to flow with, rather than to resist or stagnate in, all that is around you. Linda has the ability to become "at one" with any situation or emotion.

We decided that I would make the arrangements and that we would keep each other posted if any signals or dreams came through. I still couldn't figure out what the first symbols on my forehead meant, but I decided to take my journal, where I had drawn them, with me on the trip.

In the interim weeks, many further pictures came to my forehead to be sketched. One was the face of an old man with thick white hair, his visage covered with wrinkles. It was very difficult for me to get this image exactly as I saw it, so I wrote a note on the side of the sketch explaining that my drawing ability had fallen short of the total impression.

Another image was an alien type of face, dressed as a pharaoh and positioned next to a pyramid. He had pointed ears and a large, high forehead, a jutting pointed chin, enormous black eyes, and thin lips. Still another image was the profile of a Mayan Indian warrior with black sunbursts painted over the eyes. All these images were curious, and I knew they were leading somewhere, but I was not to see the destination yet.

On August 31, several images appeared at once. The man at the pyramid, whom I had first seen as a stick-like figure, now appeared full-face, covering most of the frontal region of my own face. His eyes were spectacular. As I drew his face, I saw great kindness in his deep brown eyes. Because of the large amount of white under his irises, I also knew that he had died young. His dark, thick eyebrows and wide-set eyes sparked something familiar in me. I knew those eyes. I had no idea why he was there, but it was obvious to me that he was coming closer. Maybe he was letting me know that, in coming closer, the time for my journey into his world was at hand.

I called Sandra, my housekeeper, to come and look at my forehead. I had learned in the past weeks that if I held my concentration, the images would stay for longer periods of time.

"Sandra, you have seen me draw while looking in the mirror. Do you see this man I have drawn? Does my forehead look any different to you?"

"No, Jamie. I see no man there. But your 'frontal' is like a bug bit you. . . here it is very red," she answered in her broken English. She lapsed into Spanish, trying to explain what she really saw. "Your eyes, they are different. The part in the middle of your forehead is raised, like you have been bumped. It came as you were looking in the mirror. Suddenly! You understand?"

Oh yes, I understood. Something dramatic was happening with my body. This was not merely an inner vision, but a physical manifestation of what the Voice had said. I had questioned many people in the field of parapsychology over the past few weeks, but none of them had ever heard of such a thing.

"Well, one day maybe someone other than myself will be able to see more than a bump or welt. Only time will tell," I thought.

A few days later, I became even more impressed with the detail forming in the forehead images. One of the images appeared to me as a warrior with a finely-etched shield who was screaming in the midst of battle. Behind him was a wall made of patterns of rocks. His head was covered by a helmet of feathers, reminding me of the shape of an old aviator's cap, with sides covering the ears. The part over the ears was made of hawk wings, and the proud head of the hawk was the crown of the helmet's crest.

In the same sitting, the face of an old Egyptian man with a fez appeared. His beard was the shape of the pharaoh's, and his shock of white hair escaped both sides of the fez.

I also saw a profile of a rather flat-faced, angular fellow with a long jutting chin and great long earlobes. He had no hair that could be seen, only a hat which reminded me of Nefertiti's. I knew that all these beings were to play a part in my coming journey, but I was at a loss as to how. I had made a note that possibly the warrior was Mayan, Aztec, or Toltec. I had also received the impression that there had been a war in that ancient city outside Morelia. In my anxiety, however, the "remembering" had become somewhat jumbled. I would have to work hard when I arrived in Mexico. I had a week to find the lost city.

Linda had been keeping me posted on her impressions. One day before we left, she called.

"Jamie, I had the strangest series of dreams this week. I was in a long golden dress and there was a belt at my waist that was a snake made of gold. The dress was pure gold, as well. I mean the metal. The mesh was like tiny scales. Each scale fit into the next one, form-fitting my body. I was led to a cave, and I was fighting with some man who was going to kill me by cutting out my heart. I saw the dagger flash as I woke up. It scared the hell out of me!"

"Maybe you are being shown a past life so you'll be prepared for the reality of it all if anything seems familiar down there," I replied. I didn't dare tell her about what the Voice had said about the sacrificial temple. I had spoken only of the city and the pyramids up until now. "What else did you dream?"

"Well, I saw you in danger. There was a flood, a fire, and an earthquake in between us. I couldn't reach you. It seemed as if you were across an unseen barrier, and that other world had you in a separate dimension."

"I may understand that one. Where we will be is in the state of Michoacán. In that state alone, there are over 250 sleeping volcanoes. The elements of earth, fire, and water are all great forces of nature, and each has a spirit. They were all present in your dream. This will be a cleansing for each of us. We will have to experience our own separate realities even though we'll be together."

"That makes sense. Each person has his or her own path to follow. I remember that tape you sent me, where you had a private session with Seth and Tom Massari. Seth said something similar. Didn't Seth say that I would have my own realizations? I seem to remember him saying that I would be a grounding force for you, but that we should discuss all that we were experiencing together."

"Yes, Linda, that's right. Seth also mentioned the medallion I would receive. The one the English psychic told me about months ago. You remember, after I'd climbed the mountain in Palm Springs."

"That should be exciting. I'd love to get a medallion from the past. Didn't you say that you remembered a life in Mexico during the time of the pyramids?"

"How could you forget? I'm still vibrating from that vision. It was back around the first of August, when the picture of the Aztec man with earrings and plumed headdress appeared on my forehead."

"Jamie, didn't you tell me that he had beads and a pendant of some kind on his chest?"

"Yeah, that's right. Why?"

"Well, I was wondering if that might be the way the original owner of the pendant looked. After all, that English psychic said he saw the spirit of a Mayan or Aztec warrior around you. That was months before. You hadn't even gone up the mountain at that time. Remember?"

"Linda, you're right. I'd forgotten that! Boy, it all seems to be tying together, doesn't it?"

I was anxious for the days to melt into a warm Mexican sun. It would be good to get back to the mystical green mountains and the ever-present serenity of the Villa Montana. I had traveled the world over and had never found any place as beautiful. It had been my retreat. The healing energy I had found in that Spanish Colonial hideaway had gotten me through my mother's death and a few other personal crises.

It was going to be tough stopping all these thoughts so that I could sleep. I had to be at Los Angeles International Airport by six a.m., but my mind kept rolling on. I could picture the rough-hewn beamed ceilings and smell the odor of fresh wood burning in the stone fireplace next to my bed. Even the smell of the oil they used to polish the antique Spanish furniture pierced my thoughts.

Monty Budd was going to be surprised to see me. We had

become friends the instant we had met. He was over eighty, and had retired in Morelia with his wife, Lois. Monty knew more about the artisans in Mexico than most of my Mexican friends. He made it his business to research every pueblo, and he knew the history of each culture. Being an octogenarian never stopped him. He was even a reporter for the *News*, the American newspaper in Mexico City. Monty had enough love for Mexico and her people to giftwrap the world. He would be a great help in my new adventure. If there was any back road in the state, he would find it.

Kurston was still living at the hotel, which was now owned by her son-in-law. It was amazing to find her in such an atmosphere. Kurston is the Marquise du Montferrier. Her son-in-law, Phillipe, is the Count de Reiset. French royalty is a curious find in the middle of Mexico, to say the least.

Kurston had been visiting in Los Angeles a month or two earlier and was fascinated by what was happening to me. I had given her a dinner party at my restaurant, and we had discussed the psychic impressions I received from her ring. When I held it, all kinds of pictures floated into my head. She had invited me to come down to the Villa, not knowing at the time what was rapidly to occur. I had never expected to be writing her so soon to tell her of our arrival, but Kurston had been delighted and had promised to take me to look for my "lost city."

It must have been the energy in those dramatic volcanoes, covered with their lush carpet of green flora, that gave my friends their vitality. Kurston was Monty's junior by only a few years, but she was one of the most beautiful women I had ever seen, of any age. Even more astonishing was the way she could drive through those mountains, as though she were in Monte Carlo on the day of the Grand Prix.

Four o'clock would come early, so I quietly put my thoughts away and resigned myself to sleep.

MEXICO

The plumed richness of the Aztec gods
    that mark a road rarely trod
        by those that quest for truth again,
            other life memories flooding in . . .

The eyes of one you do not know
    that pierce the core of your seeking soul,
        bridge the gap of time and place,
            guiding you into sacred space.

Mexico calls. . .just a heartbeat away
    with visions of pyramids, the Mayan way,
        to bless all of nature, worship the sun,
            glory in the knowledge that we are all one.

— Six —

The day finally arrived when Linda and I were to meet in Mexico City. Due to the bankruptcy of Continental Airlines, we had made some last-minute changes in our flight plans. She was flying in from Texas and was supposed to arrive a few moments before I did. Wrong again. Poor Linda had to wait in the airport for an hour before I arrived. She didn't speak a word of Spanish, and was being hit on by every available male between the ages of eighteen and eighty.

I bustled through the crowd, gave her a hug, and offered a helping hand with finding a taxi. The Geneva Hotel was our first stop. I had stayed there many times over the years and was thrilled to see that, although they were remodeling, they had kept their old furniture. This hotel had such an air about it of the way I expected Mexico to be. I would never have stayed in modern hotels. I had made that mistake once before — I might as well have been in New York. Mexico was, to me, the richness of Spain in the heart of the sacred lands of the people of the sun god. A perfect mixture of graciousness and the art of the ancients.

We ignored the smog on the way in and were very happy to see the typical joy of this proud race, as they greeted us with open hearts.

I called some friends and arranged dinner with them the following evening. We washed the road dust from our bodies, changed clothes, and went for a walk in the Zona Rosa. Linda, who had never been to the interior, was enchanted. Returning to the hotel, we learned that, when we left for Morelia in a couple of days, we would have to take a five-hour bus ride because the airplanes were no longer in service.

"Jamie, I'm glad we're taking the bus. I'm tired of not actually seeing a country when I hop from place to place. I want to see the real people. That's what we wanted to do in the first place."

"Well, you may be in for the time of your life. Some of the buses carry everything from chickens to vegetables, and it's a long way in between road stops. They don't have toilets on the bus. How's that for an adventure?" I asked, breaking into a belly laugh.

Linda's folks loved the out-of-doors, and she was used to camping. She had grown up helping them with their farms on the weekends, so this was no big deal for her, but I remembered the year before when I had nearly wet my pants before I finally got to a pit stop. The whole bus had waited for me at a non-scheduled toilet. This silly "gringa" sure was embarrassed.

We spent the next day visiting shops and artisans near the hotel. Since we expected Terí and Raul, my closest friends in Mexico, to come visit that evening with their children, we allowed our morning and afternoon to be long and leisurely.

That night we had a warm reunion. We took Linda to her first "tipico" (typical) restaurant. Even more delightful, this restaurant served the cuisine of Vera Cruz, and the night was filled with laughing, singing, and fabulous mariachis.

Raul is a fine architect and very knowledgeable about all the buildings and museums. We arranged to see the sights with Teri and him when we returned, but were sorry they couldn't accompany us to the Villa, which was where I had met them on their fifteenth anniversary. Knowing that we would return in a few days, however, our parting was sweet. The bed beckoned. Our bus would leave very early.

The busline, Tres Estrellas, was the best, and we found the trip enjoyable. As we wound our way out of the state of Mexico and into Michoacán, I began to get excited. I was able to share a great deal of history with Linda, most of it learned from Monty Budd. The time passed quickly and, arriving in Morelia, we were on our way. Energy pounded in my ears. This sleepy city was magical, with its cathedrals and legends of conquistadors. I felt that I was home.

We grabbed a taxi and were off, through town and up the hill to the Villa Montana. Just before we reached the main turn leading up the hill, I saw a high, chain-link fence to my right. I couldn't believe my eyes. Behind the fence was a camel . . . then an elephant. "Good Lord," I thought, "it's a zoo!"

Linda had noticed it, too. "Jamie, look! There's the camel and elephant from your journal!" We had zoomed past the fence by that time and were rounding the corner to the entrance. The sign, "Zoological," had a stain down the middle of its "Z" from the rusting of the iron letters imbedded in the stucco. I was thunderstruck, but it wasn't until later that I had time to think about it.

At the Villa Montana, we were shown to our room, a beautiful suite with dark tiled floors and a great stone fireplace. The sofa was a welcome sight, and I sat down to think.

"Linda, come here and look at my journal again. I just can't believe that zoo down the hill! I've been here three times and I've never seen it before. It wasn't there when I was sixteen. That was my first visit. Do you think there's a pyramid near it?"

"I'm still amazed, Jamie. It was like a sign pointing something out to us. Otherwise, you wouldn't have drawn it in your journal. Why don't we go and check it out tomorrow, okay?"

We agreed to visit the zoo the next day, took some quick baths, and called Monty.

"Monty, it's Jamie. I'm here at the Villa!"

"Don't move. I'll be right over!" Click. The phone went dead.

Well, that was a surprise. He was always coming to the Villa early in the morning, but usually his afternoons were very full. I hadn't even had time to tell him that Linda was with me. We decided to meet him on the veranda.

Monty appeared, grinning from ear to ear. After kisses and hugs, we sat down to catch up. He looked at the journal and was very interested in my latest developments. He knew me as a Cordon Bleu chef, not as a mystic, and was startled, to say the least. Kurston had stopped by to have a drink with us, and both of them were talking at the same time.

"Kurston knows about what happened in Michoacán a few months ago, girls. In a tiny village not too far from here there was a landing of some outer space folks. I believe I still have the article. They looked like beings made of light and the villagers got frightened. The villagers tried to throw rocks at them but the rocks just sailed right through them. The government is investigating because such strange things happened after the craft left the area."

"Monty is right. Did you know that the villagers had vegetables that began to grow into giant sizes? They had one carrot that weighed 200 pounds! Didn't they say that one tomato was as large as a bushel basket, Monty?"

"Kurston, if they only had pictures of it I could show these girls. The article I have showed just a cartoon-type drawing with people throwing rocks at three light beings. Those vegetables were really big. Can you imagine a tomato that weighed over a hundred pounds?"

Linda sat silently as I told them what had happened to me. We discussed where to go to find my pyramids, and Kurston offered to take us along the road to Patzcuaro in the morning. My state of excitement was like none I had ever known before.

After dinner, I retired to our suite to find out what the Voice would tell me to do next. We were both bushed. The bus ride had taken its toll. I began to meditate, saying the words I heard in my mind out loud so that Linda could hear them. We also taped everything on a cassette.

Linda had seen the pictures appear on my forehead and had watched me before when I drew them as I meditated. Now she was experiencing the situation in a new way, because we were being given actual instructions. I faithfully repeated the words.

"We want the two of you to go outside to the patio level just above you where the pool is. We will be visible at that level right now."

We grabbed our robes and house shoes and were out the door with the tape recorder. The panorama of Morelia below took my breath away. The cathedral lights had been extinguished, and the city looked like a fairy wonderland. I looked to the sky and began recording our comments.

"I wonder where they are?" I said. "Oops! I nearly fell in the flowerbed. Is the tape going? Yes, it's recording." I was in credibly nervous, answering my own questions before Linda had a chance to open her mouth. Both of us scanned the heavens.

"There they are, Linda. Look!"

"Where?"

"Over there above that triangle-like set of stars on the right, I mean the left. . .God, I'm nervous!"

"Uh-huh, I see them!"

"You see how it looks like thousands of tiny green and red lights shooting out from three different stars? They must be mother ships. They're so far away they look like stars. If they weren't moving so erratically, it would be confusing. See 'em?"

"Yeah, it looks like an energy field of little red and green lights."

"Oh my God, look at them shooting out — there must be two or three hundred. An entire armada! Have you ever experienced anything like this before?"

Linda was speechless. She just stared, her lips parted and her green eyes glowing in the midnight revelry. I told her that the Voice had started again, and then repeated the words I was hearing into the tape player. They were telling me how our planet was in great danger, including specifics about war and weapons, and organizations that wanted to control all the world's people. They also told me why they had chosen me to talk to, and why I had to pay attention. The very "family of man" would depend upon it. Love was the key.

When the Voice ended, the ships were gone. I walked back to the room in a kind of daze. We both wanted to hear the tape again, but when I went to replay it we were startled to hear a high-pitched, whirring sound in the background. It sounded as if they were right on top of us. The sound could have been the tape machine itself, but it came in irregular bursts.

The Voice had said that the message was for us alone. We listened all the way through and realized that the recording was there up until that specific message, and that it continued after that point, but that the message itself was not there. There were no skips or blanks, the message was just missing. Confidential and "just for us" meant just that! They had made sure no one would ever hear that part of the tape again.

Linda was floored. "Jamie, it's gone. It's just not there! I heard it, and I saw the tape running when you recorded it. You even checked it before."

"Linda, record what you just said onto that tape. No one would believe this if I were the only one to tell them. It has to be your voice and your own words. Otherwise they'd think I was nuts. . . totally crazy!"

After Linda had recounted this event in her own words into the tape recorder, I told her I wanted to sit in front of a mirror with just my forehead showing and see if any pictures would come to the surface of my skin. She could watch, and I would draw the pictures to see if any more clues about our journey would appear. The pictures did come, but as usual they made no sense to me since they always seemed to relate to the future. We were too dazed at that point to even discuss their possible meanings, so we opted for bed. The mixture of excitement, UFOs, mystery, and sense of adventure had us concerned that we would be unable to calm down enough to sleep, but it wasn't as hard as we expected. The trip from Mexico City had been a lifesaver after all. The sandman crept gently into the room, sprinkling us with pixie dust, and the next sounds we heard were those of the following morning.

A pink dawn and the chattering of schoolchildren floated through the handwoven cotton curtains, bringing the day. After breakfast with Monty, we realized that he was wondering if we had lost our sanity. Monty had seen the invention of the car in his lifetime, and even though he had experienced a lot, this was a bit much. I watched him saunter off, slightly shaking his head.

We had agreed to meet Kurston at her house on the back of the grounds, so we walked through the giant gates, which remained locked to guests, and across the yard. Kurston was ready to go. Her living room had a whole shelf of pre-Columbian artifacts she had found, and as I admired them, she asked which I liked most.

"That one," I said immediately, without actually looking. She picked it up and gave it to me so quickly, I didn't even know what had happened. I thanked her profusely as she grabbed some Kleenex to wrap it in and stuck it in my purse. I had always loved pre-Columbian artifacts, and this was my first to own.

I looked down at the tiny body which had been made of clay so many thousands of years ago, and was amazed to see flecks of paint on the eyes and the top curve of the necklace. Its headdress had been broken off and its eyes were very oriental looking. Its arms were covered to the elbow by clay bracelets with protruding beads. The necklace had obviously been covered at one time with bright orange paint which now remained only in the crevice of the neckline, but was worn away on the other parts. A faint remembrance of white coloring lingered around its curious eyes. Its tiny face was flanked by enormous earrings, circular and standing straight out to the side. The clay itself was a tawny golden color, very different from the red earth of Morelia. As I made my way out Kurston's door, I admired the happy expression on the face of my new little friend.

We were in the car within minutes, and headed towards Patzquaro. There were two possible roads, so we decided to go out on one and return by the other. The reason for this was that three years earlier I had been with Monty, driving to visit some local artisans, when I had seen two haystack-type things on a hill, similar to knee-high, multi-layered wedding cakes. They were covered with grass, and I found out later that they were called *yacatas*. Yacatas are small rounded pyramids, about twenty feet in circumference, which the Tolucans used as bases for the statues of their gods. Monty had said that the government had just discovered them and was planning a dig. The yacatas I had seen three years earlier had been near a fork in the road, and for most of this morning I kept looking for signs of them.

As luck would have it, I was getting more confused all the time. Nothing looked right. It had been three years since I had last seen the yacatas, and I was not remembering the way. Everything looked different.

On the return road, we stopped at a place called Tsntsun

san ("sin·soon·sohn"). It was located at a fork in the road, but the earth there was totally uncovered. I saw a high embattle-ment topped by five rounded structures — yacatas. It never occurred to me that they had been covered by grass until recently. We stopped.

I walked up to sit on top of the first level, and began to concentrate on a rock I had picked up. From where I sat, the lake at Patzquaro was far in front of me. The fields between sparkled with fuchsia and yellow wildflowers. All of a sudden, I saw the lake in my mind's eye covered by hundreds of boats, filled with warriors. The men were naked to the waist, their chests painted with various black designs. They wore wristbands of a turquoise color, and on their heads they had bright, plumed headdresses.

I could feel someone watching, and was drawn to look behind me. The top of the embattlement was covered with about seven hundred warriors. Seeing the power of the awesome painted faces of this Indian nation, I knew how Custer must have felt.

The sound of chanting came from the lake. Stronger and stronger it came, until I became a part of that call to war. "Ho Huasatecas! Ho·tol·e teca!" came the cry. The earth beneath me turned red from the blood of these mighty warriors. I wanted out. I couldn't bear it any longer. With pure strength of will, I pulled myself to a standing position. Their cries con-tinued to ring in my ears, and I nearly fell from the lower level.

Kurston was anxious to hit the road, and Linda's face sud-denly looked concerned as she approached me. I must have been totally ashen. I forced one foot in front of the other and headed to the car. The ride home was silent for a while, until finally I spoke up.

"There was a great war there in Tsntsunsan. I saw the war and how they fought to defend their homes. The lake was covered with boats from the Huastecans. The Toltecs must have been with them. This area belonged to the Tolucans. Monty told me that. What was that place, Kurston?"

"Well, it was the largest marketing center in early Mexican

history. . . before the Spaniards came. All the different Indian nations met there to exchange goods. Being centrally located, it was very valuable. They had plenty of water and fish from the lake, and rich land for crops."

Linda asked, "Jamie, do you think that was the place?"

"No. I can't really be sure, but the Voice told me I would find a buried city. The city we just saw has already been uncovered." I felt that my heart was going to break. "This is so silly. . . where in the world can it be? I guess we'll have to hire a driver and go again tomorrow. I don't want to waste any more of Kurston's time."

Linda patted my hand and told me not to worry. "We'll find it. It will be here. Don't allow yourself to get discouraged — tomorrow is another day."

After a beautiful buffet lunch at the Villa, we decided to walk to the zoo. It was a fabulous sunny day and I needed the air.

Inside the zoo, we went directly to the section abutting the main road, containing a camel and two elephants. One elephant was from India; its pen had a back wall of adobe and stucco. As we walked to the other elephant's pen, I noticed that its ears were different from the first one's. This African elephant had a point atop its ear, just like the one in my drawing. "How's that for precise?" I thought. I consoled myself for a few moments with that realization as we headed back up the hill to the hotel.

Kurston had told us over lunch that the hotel was built practically on top of a pyramid. This was even more confusing to me, as I was now being barraged with facts. I decided to review with Linda the process by which I was forming my opinions.

"Well, Linda, I guess I must be acting stupid. The set of pictures that I first drew were definitely clues. . . we found those. Now I'm confused about what happened to me today out there in Tsntsunsan. I need to find out what I'm supposed to look for, but I just can't seem to get it right. The flashes I got of what I was supposed to be looking for were those haystack things. All the rest fits with the ruins we saw today: the forked road and the warriors I saw in my head. What do you think?"

"You've got to give yourself a break, Jamie. Don't push yourself so hard. We've got several more days."

"I know we do, but if we run out of time I have to stay! I can't leave it unsettled."

"Look, Jamie, Monty told us that we can have his car all day tomorrow, and we can hire his driver. You'll find it. You know about illusions as well as I do. What appears to be real is never that way. You have to truly 'see' the life around you. You're just too stirred up right now to see with your real eyes — the ones in your heart."

"What would I do without you here? I can't tell you how much it means to me. Seth was right — you are a grounding force for me."

We began to discuss how I had psychically heard the word "Lagunillas" in relation to the old man I had drawn. He was the only real, human, modern-day person in my journal. All of my other drawings had been of spirit guides or symbols, except for this old man. The plumed warrior could have been one I had seen in my head today. The strange pharaoh had been an outer-space-looking being. I wasn't expecting to meet him!

I pulled out a map of Michoacán, surprised to find a town named Lagunillas on the road to Patzquaro. Earlier, I had thought that Lagunillas Market in Mexico City would bring me together with the old man in my drawing. Tomorrow would be the sure test of the road to Patzquaro.

The next day, Ismael, Monty's driver, waited with the car. Monty had placed us in reliable hands, which would prove to be a real asset as the day wore on.

We scoured every back road bearing a sign which indicated a pyramid, and stopped in Lagunillas to see if we would meet my mystery man. We went from there to the lake at Patzquaro, and then to the main plaza and marketplace. We took our time looking through clothing stalls, buying a few typical female pretties.

While we were looking at one set of blouses, Linda was bothered by an old woman. The little lady, no taller than four-foot-five, must have been in her late nineties. Her toothless smile and brown crumpled skin made her a pitiful but sinister figure. I spoke to her in Spanish, since Linda was hopelessly out of her element.

"How old are you, Grandmother?" I asked.

"Five," she replied. A guilty, bitter gleam in her eye flashed for a brief second, then vanished. I was unclear as to whether I had seen it at all, and then realized that I definitely had, for she began to psychically project pictures to me that were nothing like the old crone in front of us. I saw them in great clarity, and was very uncomfortable with her ability.

"Things are not always as they seem!" rang in my head. I knew that she was a *bruja*, a sorceress, in every sense of the word. She was testing me, and insisted on pulling Linda's long, golden hair. She wanted it, she said, to make money with. She was pretending to be a harmless old lady who had lost her marbles, but soon she began to pull and pinch Linda. By this time, Linda was scared.

I decided to play along for a moment or two, and pretended I was buying her act as Linda photographed us. I had delicately placed myself next to the crone, moving Linda out of harm's way. After our little photo session, I smiled and moved on to the next stall. Then I heard Linda call for help. I ran back, only to find the old witch pinching her and pulling her hair again. If she hadn't been toothless, she probably would have bitten Linda, just to see what kind of stuff I was made of. She knew exactly which buttons to push and how to make me angry. I pictured what the crowd would do if they saw this helpless old woman being thrown aside by a young, healthy "gringa." The possibilities offered no reassurance.

I quickly separated the old bat's hand from Linda's hair and decided that the best way out of this situation was the path of least resistance — to run! Clamping my hand on Linda's forearm, I dragged her back toward the main plaza.

"Linda, she's a witch, a black witch of the worst variety. Let's get out of here. I'm in no condition to fight whatever she's got up her sleeve."

Rounding the corner at top speed, trying to avoid the

crowd, I looked back to see her cackling at me. She was no dummy. She could see my luminous body. It was full of holes made by my confusion.

The astral body becomes luminous when it is activated by psychic energy that has traveled up the spinal column. Seers can see this body and tell if persons are in their power or not. In this instance, I was on the edge of psychic overload and had blown too much energy through my body, so my protection was not in place. It was one hell of a time to run into a group of sorcerers! The confusion had made me weak, and I had over-compensated by funneling too much energy up to my third eye to help me figure out what was happening. Terrific! Now I was supposed to protect both Linda and myself.

I had made sure that the old crone didn't have any of Lin-da's hair in her hand before we flew around the corner, because if she had, she could have used it to attack either of us by putting it on a voodoo doll or using it in a witch's potion. There were thousands of things that could befall someone if a sorcerer obtained personal fingernail clippings, hair, or a piece of their clothing. I had to get us out of the street market, and fast.

The boardwalk in front of the indoor market was jammed with people, and I tried to put as much space as possible be-tween us and the old crone. I had Linda by the wrist and we were walking fast.

"Jamie, stop! There's your old man, look at him!"

"Where?" I mumbled. People were staring at us, so Linda dropped to a whisper.

"You nearly ran over him. He's right behind us, kneeling. He's begging with his hat in his hands. I think he's blind."

I swung on my heel and looked at the old man's back, moving around him to see his face. If his hat had been on his head, Linda never would have recognized him. Looking at his face, I began to cry.

It was the same man that I had drawn. His humble atti-tude of prayer, with his hat in his hands, his worn and frayed cotton pants, and his soiled white cotton shirt, hit me hard. I felt guilty that I had been blessed with so much. His serape was a cushion for his knees, and I wanted deeply to lift him up and hug him, to tell him that he was loved. I wanted him to know that someone would remember him in her prayers, and that that someone was me.

Slow tears melted into silent rivers and etched their way down my face. Everyone was staring at me. I couldn't make a move to hug him or touch him without feeling like I was going to embarrass us both, so instead I quickly jumbled through my purse and grabbed some money. That was one way I could help him, even if it was only for a short time. Inside myself I was afraid that someone would rob him, since he couldn't see what I was about to put into his sombrero. I would have to let him know in some way, so I stuffed a twenty-dollar bill in his hands, telling him in Spanish what it was.

I was nearly bawling when Linda grabbed my arm and dragged me to the corner. She never raises her voice, but she was very firm this time.

"Jamie, look at me! You just got through with one situation that wasn't what it seemed to be. Maybe this one isn't either."

"You're right," I mumbled through fast-drying tears. "I just feel so helpless when I see someone in that condition. Did you see those two guys laughing at him?"

"Of course I did. For all you know they may be laughing at the two of us for being so stupid. How do you know that they aren't apprentices of that supposedly blind man?"

"I hadn't thought of that," I said, suddenly furious. I ran a few steps back to see the blind man. He was gone. So were the two that had been laughing.

Ismael was waiting as we rambled up to the car, emotionally exhausted. "Let's go," I said, as he took the last lick of his frozen fruit ice. We were off to Tsntsunsan. I'd be jiggered if I was going to let these Mexican sorcerers get the best of me! I was royally teed off. Now there was fire in my blood. I was going to get through this even if one of those volcanoes blew!

The ruins looked like double silhouettes in the hot mid-afternoon sun, and waves of heat slammed against my face as I began the long climb to the top of the hill. Linda followed with the camera, and I translated the history as Ismael talked. When we reached the summit, Ismael led us to an opening in the back of the second yacata.

"This was recently discovered by our archaeologists. It was a real find. It's the entrance to a sacrificial temple."

My mind flew in a hundred directions at once. Had I heard him correctly? My body had been hot; now it was ice-cold. I hurriedly told Linda what we were standing next to, and her expression became one of smiling knowingness.

From below, the entire embattlement had seemed like a giant wall, grey-black with a rusty color mixed in here and there. Up closer, as I had discovered the year before, it was made of lava-rock bricks that had pieces of slate wedged between them instead of mortar.

These ruins had once been a great marketing and trading center for many tribes in central Mexico. In order to fortify it, the people had built a huge retaining wall along its front border, which was about thirty feet high. A picture of this wall had appeared on my forehead, and I had drawn it next to an ancient warrior with a helmet crowned by a hawk's head. He was running and screaming war calls in front of the wall. I had not seen the yacatas in that picture, but now as I looked to my right I could see them clearly — solid, physical, and magnificent.

Each rounded yacata was like a stack of plates, slightly larger in diameter at the bottom. The hole I was looking down, where the archaeologists had started digging out the entrance to the temple, was stairless, but the side walls were slightly graduated at the bottom. I supposed that this had been done to stabilize the walls, since no mortar had been used.

Ismael continued, "You see the way the bottom is covered with cement? That's because the archaeologists ran out of money."

"Linda," I cried, "we've hit pay dirt! This is the place! I just can't believe it. Let's go exploring!"

"It would be better if you go on your own. You'd be able to think better that way. Just be careful. I'm going to take some pictures and find my own quiet time, okay?"

"All right. I'm going to head toward the road to see why I
was wrong about the temple entrance being behind the third
pyramid. I guess if the Voice had said yacatas, I never would
have understood."

"But Jamie, it *is* behind the third one! There are five
pyramids. You came up the front of the embattlement and are
now in the middle of it. Look behind you. There are two more
behind this wall. If you walk toward the back side about twenty
feet or so, you can see it all. This is just like your vision."

She was right, there were five. I must have been looking
backwards. I headed for the back side of the embattlement.

A soccer field was nestled in the green undergrowth
behind the ruins. As I gazed at it, it began to peel back its
modern-day covering, and I saw an ancient city filled with
people. It looked like some of the pictures from my childhood
Sunday School class. The walls were like a maze. Then, as
quickly as the vision had appeared, it vanished.

So this was it. I would talk to someone from the
archaeology department in Mexico City. Maybe Terí and
Raul's cousin, Laura, would know something about this place.
She had worked here as an anthropologist a few years back.

For the next few days, we went down to the pyramid below
the hotel. So much digging had occurred there that the owner
of the land had built a protective wall around it, but part of
the structure lay outside his property line, so we sat there and
meditated a bit. Finally, frightened that we would get into
trouble, we decided to forget about digging there.

The rest of our time was spent exploring the markets in
Morelia and visiting points of interest with Monty. On our last
afternoon we visited the main cathedral, which I had been to
before. It was one of the oldest in Mexico, its entire facade
covered in goldleaf. Linda and I went inside to see the
beautiful statue of the Virgin Mary. High above the Virgin's
shrine, we noticed carvings in the wood, forming a house-like
enclosure for the statue. Since neither of us had been raised
Catholic, we didn't really understand any of the symbolism.

My eyes, following the golden structure to the very top of

the ceiling, suddenly dilated. There, high above all the other gold carvings, was a white marble cloud, five inches thick and sculpted three-dimensionally. In its center was an Egyptian-type pyramid, pointed, with an eye in its upper portion just like on the American dollar bill.

I quickly told Linda what I was seeing. We crossed to the other side of the cathedral to see if there was another one above the shrine for Joseph.

"Linda, our dollar has the same symbol. The reason is that our country was founded on a search for freedom, and on the belief that every man and woman had the right to find the Creator on their own. You know those words in Latin above the pyramid on the dollar?"

"Well," I continued as she nodded, "they mean 'new order of the ages.' The founding fathers knew, even then, that one day every person would come to be at one with the Source. America was the hope for all people to find that freedom. Our Age of Aquarius or New Age was starting to form even that long ago. Most of our founders were Freemasons and had to work in secret. They were the builders of our country."

"That might be why you are being given all this information, Jamie. The Voice said that the time was now, remember?"

"Sure, but what in the world is that symbol doing in this cathedral, which was build in the late 1500s? The Catholic Church has always refused to allow its members to be Masons. Maybe there was a secret society of Masons here, and the Holy Roman Church has never known that the symbol was here. . . after all, it is higher up than any of the other symbols in the entire church. Originally, Freemasons were a secret order of men interested in uncovering the hidden or occult secrets of the universe so that humanity could be free to live in harmony and abundance, without control by the Catholic Church. The Church had stolen all of the original manuscripts set down by the early disciples, and had entered into partnership with the aristocracy to control the economy and all the people.

"The American founding fathers, like Ben Franklin and Thomas Jefferson, were Masons. In the 1600s, the Masons collected all their secret data and smuggled it out of Europe to a location in the United States. Marie Bauer Hall has been working on a site in Williamsburg, Virginia since 1932, and has decoded much information that has given her the exact location. Support for her work is mounting, and financial donations are helping it along. This secret data will be revealed soon, so that the world will know, when the New Age begins, that they no longer need to be controlled."

"That could be," Linda said. "All I know is that we are supposed to find it. It certainly tells me that all religions are founded on something very basic. We, as people, had to come from some inner knowledge of our true roots, and we have been seeking for meaning to life since Day One. The secrets that the builders of the pyramids took with them have to be the answer."

"Actually Linda, I believe that the secrets are within each of us. That eye up there is the one eye which each of us has that will help us see what the world is really like. To do that, we have to use the eye of our heart of hearts." Linda and I emerged at that point into the burning mountain sun.

We ducked into a tiny cafe for a cold soda. As we sipped through old-time paper straws, I said, "I guess that's what I should be doing right now — looking with my heart of hearts. I can't help but feel that I've been slow finding the answer to why I was sent on this trip. The Voice never said that I was supposed to have some huge experience, but I'm not putting it all together into one whole picture. I feel fragmented."

"We still have lots to do in Mexico City, and when it's all over you will have the whole picture. You know that nothing is ever clear if you don't have all the pieces, Jamie. Be patient. That's a lesson in itself."

Talk turned to other subjects on our way to the Villa for a last evening with our friends there. Our train would leave at midnight, and early the following morning we would be greeting Raul and Teri back in Mexico City.

After many thanks and hugs all around, we went to the station to find our "dormitorios." These one-person sleeping cabins had been salvaged from the States when Americans no longer traveled so much by train. I loved them! Everything but the bed was miniature. It was a miracle that all my luggage fit into the tiny space.

The stars and moonlight bathed the lumbering Michoacan mountains in ethereal light. The part of me that belonged to those mountains tore at my insides to stay. The sadness in Linda's face surprised me. She felt it too. It was like leaving an old, old friend.

Rails were popping; we blended our own energy with the melody of the whistles and the clacking of the train. The tarched sheets welcomed my body, but my mind refused to dismiss the familiar sights and sounds that had nurtured me over the past six days.

Both Linda's door and mine were closed, but I could feel her thinking across the corridor. What had she felt during the journey so far? The part of her which the divorce had stifled was apparent in her quietness at times. She had been hurt deeply, and was even now holding some of her thoughts from active consciousness. I had hoped that this trip would be the key for her — the budding of the Jericho rose. Just like that wondrous plant, she had rolled across the desert floor and wound up into herself. The Jericho rose could go for years without water, without dying, but when it rained the rose would once again plant its roots and turn from brown to green, opening the leaves that had been curled into itself.

I prayed that something would show Linda how to find herself again. The hurt could be healed only with time, and this was a journey of discovery for her, as well as for me.

The morning train station was a sight to behold. Everyone on our train piled off with goods for the market and babies tied neatly across their breasts with "rebozos." The men straightened their "vacaro" hats, which bore a tiny tassel at the back that was the only symbol of their origin and was particular to the state of Michoacan. With truckfuls of luggage, porters bustled through engine steam to find their ways to the dock. The deafening chatter was a wonderful welcome.

Sruggling through the mob, we found Raul and Terí, all smiles and kisses. We rode to the Geneva Hotel to deposit our bags, and were off to the Museum of Anthropology.

We could have chosen many sections of the museum, but each was a complete three-hour tour. We finally decided on the one highlighting ancient cultures.

In a room featuring a huge fresco of Aztec religious symbols, Linda grabbed my arm, pointing to the highest portion of the wall above us.

"Jamie, there's the bat and the mask you drew the night we saw the saucers in Morelia!"

"Where?" I asked, scanning the near-surrealistic painting.

"Up there on the right. Take a picture of it for your journal. It's further proof of your drawings."

She was right! There they were! I asked the guide about the symbolism of the horrible-looking bat face. She replied that it was a symbol of reincarnation, an integral part of the Aztec belief system. I was thrilled at the possible meaning of this clue to my personal journey. Since the bat was an ancient symbol of reincarnation, perhaps I had lived here before and was coming back to reclaim the secrets of the ancient ones — the ones who had originally colonized these civilizations deep in Mexico's heartland.

In the next room we found an ancient piece of obsidian, used as a scalpel for operations by the early nations. I suddenly realized that it was the exact shape I had drawn that same night. It almost looked like a seahorse shape, but was quite a bit fatter.

The guide's voice floated my way as I took a snapshot of that piece. "Ladies and gentlemen, I would like you to look at the various obsidian knives we have here in these cases. The rounded ones were used for healing. These were used to open the scalps of our ancient warriors so that pressure could be removed from the brain. If a warrior had received a wound to the head in battle, the skull fragments could be removed. We find that brain surgery was quite common among the ancients, and really quite successful. Over here you will see a skull that was repaired long before the person died. The skull shows that the newer bone had filled the orifice made by some blunt object, and the carbon-dating method has proven. . ."

Her voice trailed away as I sank deeply into my previous vision of the panorama at Tsntsunsan. I had found tiny pieces of obsidian chips at the base of a cornfield near the embattlement. They were very old, Ismael had said.

Had that been a sign that we, as people, healed all things, even though our brothers and sisters tried to destroy one another? I felt that healers were parts of history who had always existed to balance the destruction. Was I supposed to be a part of the balance for light and love in my twentieth-century world?

Before I realized what was happening, we were back at the entrance. The rain had begun, as it almost always did in the afternoons. It was a mad dash to the car. Our day had begun at five a.m, so we decided to rest and see Raul and Terí in the morning.

Linda was pensive as we finally settled in the room. "Jamie, do you remember seeing the Templo Mayor this morning? You know, the main temple of the Aztecs? Well. . . if we had been here before now, we wouldn't have seen it totally uncovered. I don't think there was any accident in our being here at this exact time. When I saw the statue of the reclining figure with a bowl on his belly, something shot through me like a sharp icicle. He was the god that caught the hearts that had been cut from victim's chests. I just went cold all over and felt faint."

"I know what you mean — it must have been some flash from the past. The god's name is Chacmool. I can't imagine how all those years of blood didn't leave stains. Parts of the statue still had the original paint." I guessed that this was because it had been buried in the earth. Since Mexico City is on top of a lake, the earth is red-brown and damp, and maybe this had soaked out the blood, or perhaps the archaeologists had cleaned it.

"Jamie, I just know that I had to have been in a precarious situation back then. My dream, the chills, the fear, it was all too real for me to put aside. I've seen that god's face before — it's all too close for me to feel comfortable."

"I know how you feel. That's how I felt when I saw the planet being exploded in the movie *Star Wars*, years ago. I was crying uncontrollably and had to go to the lobby. I had seen that happen somewhere, sometime, long ago. . .you just know it's true. Something deep inside of you breaks and the flood of emotions that comes to the surface is scary as hell."

"I need to get some air. How about a walk down to the court on the street where the artists are?"

On the way out, we lingered in the lobby to look at some fabulous paintings that had been there since I was a child, salvaged from a bulldozed church. The gilt and burgundy frames were stories high. I had often wondered whether they had built the lobby around those priceless oil renderings. They were scenes of nobles surrounded by various angels, all depicted around the time of Maximilian and Charlotta. Napoleon's little nephew had done all right for himself!

Just looking at the paintings separated us from the lingering thoughts of Aztec brutality. Night air and music and pantomime from the street players completed this transition.

We planned an early start with Terí, Raul, and the children. Terí's cousin, Lulie, was a great guide for Linda, since she spoke perfect English and was very knowledgeable about all of the ruins. We looked forward to the next day.

PYRAMIDS

How profound,

       how ambiguous you are,

        like a field of windswept wheat.

Beyond the unutterable distance of time,

  lies the trust you found so blindly false.

      Now. . .there is no room for me in your silence.

  I must carefully sift the thoughts I give you.

   Discarding the chaff,

           storing the grain.

  In the balance,

      I strive for some peace of mind,

       however minute

        in comparison to this emptiness.

      But I could never sell the memory of you,

       even in your somber silence. . .

      Not for gold,

       not for silver,

        not even for an eternity in heaven.

— Seven —

Driving to the pyramids at Teotihuacan, I remembered another time, another life. One of the beings from another civilization, who had been on this planet to love and teach the people here, had been my teacher. I saw brief flashes of times when he was gone. I would sit and talk to the pyramids, hoping he would return. That love was being rekindled as I came closer to the pyramid site.

The flashes had been so brief that I hadn't been able to form a cohesive image. I just felt the sadness inside growing, together with my longing to see the pyramids again.

If I talked to those beings now, I wondered, could they answer? I was deep in thought, trying to remember some clue, but nothing came as we passed the fields of corn and autumn-gold grass. There was an occasional mesquite tree or field of maguey, but the scenery was not particularly exciting. Linda and Lulie discussed Aztec history, and I let my thoughts wander to the place of power I hoped to discover within myself.

The giant pyramids of the sun and moon were waiting for us as our VW van pulled into the parking area. Crossing the lot to the entrance, we came upon a pole about three stories high. At its top were five men in the costumes of their native state, Veracruz. The Indians were dressed as they had been back in the days before Cortez. Their bright colors flashed in the breeze as each of them spoke words to the gods for protection. Four of them, dressed mainly in red hues, descended the pole and swung freely from giant ropes attached to their feet.

All four ropes were tightly wound around the pole, and would be controlled to some degree by the Indian still on top. He was chanting and playing a small percussion instrument I had never seen before. The flying bodies of the four men then began to swing out over the crowd. As their ropes unwound and they neared the end of their flight, their heads zoomed dangerously close to the ground.

Had any one of them panicked, the others would have been slung to the ground. Each man had sung his personal song to the god Mescalito as he flew.

The Indians solicited donations for their exhibition, and I took one aside.

"Excuse me, Señor, do you sing to Mescalito for protection?"

"Yes, Señorita, in a way. It is truly to remind us of how our own songs blend in with the songs sung by *all* things. It is for this reason that we are allowed to fly. The spirit is taken from us when we perform this task — we are our true selves once again. The body no longer exists for us. However, if we do not return to our bodies in time, we will remain with the spirit world, for our heads would be crushed on the earth below."

"Do you ever feel it is just a show. . . for the tourists, I mean?"

"Oh no, Señorita, I fly to make my living, but it is with the knowledge that I am reminded of my oneness with the universe. If I forgot the truth in oneness, I would deserve to die."

"You, my friend, are blessed. The world could learn much from you. Thank you. I must go now," I said, and ran to catch up with the others.

I was richer by far for having talked to that beautiful Indian man. The money I donated could never pay for the knowledge I received. I was only a cell in the body of the universe, my journey one of finding weakness and harmony with the rest of the body of All That Is. I was looking for all the parts of the key to open that door forever, but the key was fragmented.

I allowed myself to be taken on a quick tour by Lulie before I spoke up.

"We have to leave tomorrow, and I really want to go searching on my own. I haven't gotten the medallion yet, and maybe I'll find it digging around in the brush back there. After all, Seth said I would find it close to some pyramids. Do all of you want to go too?"

Teri spoke first. "That would be a great adventure. I know the children would love it. Just remember that it's forbidden to dig on the grounds. If you find anything, be quiet about it. I don't want any of us to get into trouble."

Raul Jr. and I started out in the field behind the Pyramid of the Moon and fooled around for twenty minutes or so with no luck. I began to hear human voices and left the arroyo as quickly as I could, scratching my foot on a fallen mesquite branch.

It was Marianna, Teri's daughter, with Linda. They were haggling with two young men who kept glancing nervously over their shoulders.

"Hey, Linda, what are you up to? What are they selling?" I called.

I was silenced with a finger to the lips by Marianna. Oops, I had forgotten. These were some of the many young people who dug up artifacts and sold them on the sly.

Raul Jr. and I began to examine the artifacts being sold by the boys, discussing their authenticity. Linda decided that she didn't care if they were fakes, and she made her buy. I chose a bead and three little heads, very pleased with myself. I still wanted to look for my medallion. I had been told by a psychic I knew that it might be near a bazaar. The whole area was surrounded by shops, so this could be the spot. We decided to catch up with Teri, Raul, and Lulie so that we could all go together. We all were very hot, and apparently they had been scouting for shade as they waited for us. I ran ahead and bought us all some ice cream. What a welcome relief!

After scouting through a few shops with no luck, we decided to call it a day and head for a nearby restaurant which, Raul guaranteed, was cool.

"La Cueva" was a surprise. Built inside a natural cavern, there must have been a couple of hundred steps leading down to the restaurant floor. I was chatting with Teri as we entered, and hadn't noticed that Linda was lagging behind.

When we were seated, I looked at her face sharply. She was ashen, and the muscle in the side of her cheek twitched. Her hands were trembling, and her eyes were wide with fear. . . could it be fear?

The kids were snapping pictures of all of us, and I could see that Linda was forcing her smiles. Had she been sitting closer to me, I could have spoken sooner, but she quickly excused herself and left the table. I caught her about ten feet away.

"Linda, are you okay? You look like you saw a ghost."

"I did, Jamie. This is the place. I was murdered here! This is the place in my dream! I have to see if the area back there has another smaller cave. I know this is it."

"Do you want me to go with you? Will you be all right?"

"This is something I have to do alone. I appreciate your concern, but this is my responsibility. . . to myself."

I returned to the table and relayed what had occurred to the others. Terí rolled her eyes and began to shiver.

"OOoooo. . . this gives me the shakes. How can she go alone? I'd be scared to death. I guess I'm just not that brave," she said.

I followed Linda with my eyes. She was about fifty feet in front of me. Suddenly, she dipped from sight. "Oh, dear God," I thought, "it's really there. She found it."

I knew better than to think I had cornered the market on psychic experiences, but this was the first time this kind of thing had happened to Linda.

Linda is gentle and kind, and never fights or argues in anger — she has more discipline than that. I could see that out of that cave would one day rise a total person — healed and repaired from earlier wounds. I kept glancing that way, but she didn't resurface. I was aware of how her quiet strength had protected her from near-insanity during marriage to an alcoholic who was irrational about her beauty and jealous of any friend she had. Near the end of their marriage, he had accused her of pandering to men while she was out shopping with her mother and a nine-year-old cousin. I was thankful she had survived such emotional abuse!

Just as I was fumbling with my chair to go look for her, she reappeared. Her camera still trembled a bit in her hand, but her color was returning, and her smile seemed a little more stable.

"I saw the golden dress in my mind again, and where I'd fought with that priest. I took some pictures, just to remind me that this is real. After all, the dream was very real, but this was physical proof for me," Linda said. The subject was too heavy for the luncheon situation, so I patted her hand as the conversation turned to another subject.

In minutes, we were all laughing. The reason for this was the story I was relating about my experience with Linda on the bus to Morelia. I had told Linda that the Mexicans used all kinds of manure on their crops. We had seen corn in Michoacán that was at least eleven feet, and often fifteen feet, high. The ears were enormous. It was similar to mule corn, which is very large — about four inches in diameter and more than a foot long — and is grown to feed animals back in Texas.

"But Jamie, this corn is huge. Why does it get so big?" she had asked.

"Well," I had explained, "it could be the altitude, or the kind of corn they use, but I know one real difference."

"What's that?" she had asked, turning back to the road to examine the field we were passing.

"Do you smell that awful smell? It's like open sewage, isn't it?"

"You can say that again," she had replied, wrinkling her button nose.

"Linda, that is the cheapest fertilizer available down here. Waste not, want not. Get the picture? Everything eaten is just recycled."

"Do you mean they use human...ahh..."

"Sure do," I had replied.

That had been days ago, and now everywhere we went, if that odor was present, Linda looked for the cornfields.

We were all laughing so hard that tears streamed down our cheeks. Linda was giggling hysterically. I caught my breath long enough to spit out another sentence.

"I have never seen anyone so interested in corn or fertilizer!"

That started another wave of hysterics, and we were all doubled over. It was true, but her reaction had been expressed with the keen eye of a farmer's daughter, not the elegant lady she had become. That would be one to tell when we got home!

Our final night was spent at Terí and Raul's home for a lovely dinner with "los abuelos," the grandparents. What a wonderful trip it had been; what a pity we had to leave.

Linda cried at the airport and wouldn't say goodbye. She hates saying goodbye. I cried too. This had been something neither of us could ever forget. I left first, and tried to put it all together on the plane home.

Terí's cousin Laura, the anthropologist, had told me that a city lay under the soccer field in Tsntsunsan, or at least it was suspected. She had also told me that the figure Kurston had given me was made 600 years before the birth of Christ. I was impressed.

But I felt a funny sadness creeping into my solar plexus about not finding my medallion. For this reason alone, the trip felt like it had not been a total success. There was a vague shadow hanging over the richness of what I had learned, and I didn't know why.

It had been amazing. Why was I beating myself over the head? I just couldn't figure it all out. I was too close to it in terms of time. Everything had happened so very fast. Maybe I could digest the facts after I listened to the tapes I had made, and looked over the notes in my journal. I had some photos which would add to my understanding once they were developed. I just felt very unsettled.

CANDLELIGHT AND LOST ANGELS

I've been a part of candlelight as long as I can remember,
    I bathed in it as often as I could,
I sat ceaselessly watching
    as it flickered in the eyes of my love,
But it has made me believe in things,
    I know don't exist. . .
The unicorns and satyrs that dance in my dreams
    are real now. . .
        Love is alive. . .
           And I am free. . .

— *Eight* —

My first five days back in Los Angeles had been quite extraordinary. I was psychically overloaded with energy, and had blown out several lightbulbs in my house simply by touching the switch to turn them on or off. The electromagnetic field around my body had become highly charged, and I gave people shocks when I touched them. It wasn't static electricity; I had hardwood floors in my home.

When I drove to see the ocean one evening, I had been stunned by the effect I was having on my car. The windshield wipers started of their own accord, as did the radio. The rock station that blasted my senses was one that I never listened to, and I was a bit frightened until the Voice came to me to explain what was occurring.

"You have assimilated much psychic energy. It had to be discharged in some way. You are like an antenna now. The energy will diminish over the next two weeks."

The appliances and radios and lights returned to their normal functions after a few days. The objects on the bookcase stopped falling off, and life began to settle into its normal routine. As this psychic energy began to taper off, I realized that all beings have power within themselves which they often refuse to recognize. This energy can be funneled if they are willing to drop the fear of it.

By that time, two weeks in Hollywood had yanked me back into the "real" world, and things were once again in a hectic state at work. Several shows and newspaper articles on fine dining kept the business flourishing. I didn't find time to quietly review my thoughts about the Mexico trip until the end of October.

Monday was my only night off, and had become a very precious time to me. I had spent the last several Monday evenings musing over the whys and wherefores of the occurrences in Mexico.

The little artifacts were particularly very special. Holding each of them in my hand, I tried to piece together my memories of the trip. One evening, as I held the one Kurston had given me, the Voice began to speak: *"Get the journal."* That was all. How strange, I thought.

Leafing through the pages, I turned to the plumed Aztec or Mayan warrior, sitting cross-legged. How beautiful he seemed to me now! I had genuine respect for the history represented in his costume.

I was still holding the artifact in my hand when the phone rang. I laid the tiny figure on my journal and reached for the receiver. As soon as I finished saying, "Sorry, wrong number," I noticed the two images, my drawing and the artifact, peering at me from the page. They were so similar, I jumped. I began to examine the two very closely. This was crazy. Now it was obvious to me why I had never noticed it before. The figure had been broken from the hips downward, and its top was missing. Only the face, arms, and chest remained. From a rough piece of clay which remained across the forehead, I could see where the plumes had been. The beads I had drawn around the neck were the same. So were the arm bracelets. The pendant I had drawn around the neck was not present on the artifact.

"What in the world could this mean?" I wondered. The Voice began to speak in my muddled brain. *"This is your medallion. Wear it well. Mount it for all to see. It is the medicine of past existences that will bring you power. The medallion will return to the maker at your death. Until that time, it is yours to watch over."*

I sat very quietly, in total awe. This was a little bit too weird! At the same time, it could be the key to understanding the drawings and the other artifacts.

I grabbed the other two artifacts I had bought at the pyramids and went through the pages of the journal. The alien-looking pharaoh matched one of them! I had drawn pointed ears on the figure's head. They didn't appear on the clay head in my hand, but as I looked closer, I realized that there were broken parts on each side of the tiny skull. The head had no ears, but the broken places could have been the areas where the ears had been. The cranium was shaped very strangely. The jaw was rather elongated and the forehead protruded, giving an almost crescent shape to the skull. My drawing had a protrusion on the front of the headdress in that shape, but I had thought that it was some kind of ornamentation — not a cobra, but something similar. How very odd it was to be looking at the two, side by side!

At the time I had done the original drawing, I had given the pharaoh pointed ears like Mr. Spock on Star Trek. He was very alien looking. I glanced at some notes that I had scrawled in my journal: the Voice had told me that the ancient predynastic pharaohs were from outer space. This was proof positive that the Indian cultures of central Mexico knew this fact as well.

I quickly turned a few more pages to compare the other drawings with the remaining clay piece. None matched. The head was flat, with a turban-type of headpiece shaped like the top of a V. The whole head was formed in that shape, with a pointed chin at the bottom. The features of the face were rather flat, and the mouth was simply a pressed, thin line. If there was any expression at all, it had to be the round, heavy-lidded eyes.

Well, two out of three wasn't bad. I started daydreaming, and turned this last head to the side in my hand, noticing the profile. That was it! I had been looking at it from the front, but it was the profile I had drawn. When I held the face at a profile angle, it made almost exactly the same shadow against the page as my sketch.

I was beginning to feel like the most unaware person in the world. Why hadn't I noticed the resemblance of these artifacts to my drawings before? I felt so utterly ridiculous. The stupidity of it all, and the beating I had given myself, thinking the trip unsuccessful, was like bile in my mouth.

I guess I came by this self-bludgeoning naturally. I often gave myself a super hard time to make sure that what others said or thought of me was not true. The psychic in Los

Angeles had told me I was fantasizing and wouldn't be a good channel or clairvoyant unless I studied with him. The people from my home town just thought I was lying when I was a child and talked of going out of my body. The jealous and the ignorant had made me hard on myself for good reason. I had to fight an internal war between the real world and the other realms I knew, and to be able to experience them both without losing the desire to live or keep my sanity. It was tough enough without having to deal with people who thought you were nuts or, worse still, "of the devil" because you could transcend their reality. I had help now: the Voice that was always with me, in feeling if not in words. It gave me great strength.

I was relieved that the Voice had finally hit me over the head and forced me to realize the truth. My faith in the guidance I had received was being strengthened. I couldn't wait to call Linda, and when I did, she was so happy. It was a victory of great importance to me. I knew then that the trip had been a great lesson.

I had to chuckle over what had occurred with my confusion, my internal war, my trying too hard and my expectations. It had taught me that I wanted more than anything to prove to myself and the world that I had a right to experience the magic in life, and that our new frontiers are those of both worlds: the physical and the spiritual. These two worlds are really one; the only boundaries we actually have are those we impose upon ourselves when we believe that things can't be done. I had bought into so many other people's answers and opinions that half of my confusion and doubt came from preconceptions, misconceptions, and the fear that those who sought to change me were right and I was wrong. I was finally learning to trust my heart. That was my greatest achievement, and my discoveries were physical proof that I could still have icing on the cake because I was doing it my way.

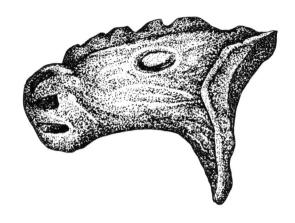

INFINITY DANCE

Open yourself to creation,
　　give of yourself for free,
　　　　live forever in the present,
　　　　　　the abundance lives within thee.
Judge not the steps you are taking,
　　each pilgrim has to find the way.
　　　　Learn to allow the eternal blossoming,
　　　　　　and darkness will give way to day.
You are creating the movements,
　　as the dance brings you closer to dawn,
　　　　each life is but a reflection
　　　　　　of infinity. . . as it waltzes along.

— *Nine* —

The months following the Mexico trip in the fall of 1982 were filled with long hours of work and attempts to carve out enough private time to jam my head full of every piece of information I could find on world religions and metaphysics. My businesses kept me in tune with the physical world, and the books kept me occupied with the realm which had become my second home.

The changes in me were subtle but very powerful, and I began to notice that I was catching glimpses from the corner of my eye of a life that I had never before dreamed possible. One day when I was reading, I saw something move with my peripheral vision. Thinking a sheet of paper had fallen from my desk, I reached to pick it up, still watching the book in front of me, and discovered that my arm had become transparent! Actually, part of it was just not there. I jumped and looked at it directly, and it was solid again. I was perplexed, to say the least, and was determined to find out what was going on.

I began to understand that humans perceive much more than we allow ourselves to believe, because we are so habituated to using our eyes in the physical sense. The solidity that we perceive is more than an illusion we have created by our agreement that it is so. When I looked at objects peripherally, I could see non- physically — solids began to move!

My living room walls were white, and the colors invested in the spectrum of purest white began to surface on them. I would look at a wall and find that it had a changing and moving surface. The physical universe was being recreated in front of my eyes; I could see atoms move!

I began contacting certain authorities in parapsychology, only to find that nobody had heard of pictures appearing on the outside of someone's forehead. The consensus was that it was very unusual, since most clairvoyants see things as pictures in their minds' eyes, or around and about them.

I began to think about the way in which the cells separated in my skin, and how they regrouped and changed color. This was the fourth dimension or density. The Voice had used the word density, explaining that the atoms in higher dimensions are less dense, and move more rapidly. The "solidity" of life was stepping aside so that I could see what wondrous truths are available to each and every person who truly wants to know the secrets of the universe. They are all there. It is inside our own consciousness that the secrets lie.

The trick to this is to be able to hold your mind at bay. Not one stray thought should be present — just a clean and clear channel for the information to come into your consciousness. This has been called "stopping the world," which is really what it is. If you can stop the chatter in your thought processes, you can stop the world. Because there are no thoughts of your own, the answers from the Creator, or Universal Force, are able to enter.

Persistence and concentration were the keys for me. I just decided to do this, and I did it. That is not really as easy as it sounds, because I had to make the time, set aside the worries of running two businesses, and learn to be comfortable and at peace with myself. It was very light at first, but as the days passed, I concentrated more on gazing and not focusing. In this way, I could see more movement.

It was during these months that the Voice came again and again. I was told to begin classes, to teach. I was scared silly, because I had no idea what to teach. The Voice implied that all the words would be heard by me and that I would just repeat them to the class.

As I began to make business decisions which would allow me the time to do this, my life became total bedlam. I sold the restaurant concept to a corporation and closed the catering company. I relinquished all the remaining equipment and finally quit the businesses totally to devote myself to psychic study and work, which would lead me into the world of other dimensions.

During this time of closing my businesses, the Voice came

to me, outlining the next steps which would free me to find my true place in life.

I don't understand how I accomplished what I did, because it took either blind faith or sheer foolishness, but it happened.

One evening, after a long day of packing up the final things from my office and moving them home, the Voice came to me.

"Your next initiation will be high in the Andes in Peru. Make your plans. There are three doorways to space. In these locations, the dimensions of ethers are not as solid."

"But what do you want me to do there? I just need to know. I guess I'm curious; please tell me," I replied.

"The treasures of wholeness and oneness are given to those who follow their own knowingness. These are the souls who find the answers to the secrets of being. You are one planet, one people, and yet you are all threads of a tapestry woven by the Creator. In your life, you will find this harmony if you are unafraid to see it."

"Will you be there to guide me?"

"Have we ever left your side? Do you not see that each time you take the moments necessary to listen, we are there?"

"I know you are right. I don't even know what to call you other than my friends."

"We are just another part of the Creator's universe. We are beings that are of service to those who would look to really see. That is enough for now. As long as your heart is pure and your intentions are full of love, you will be blessed. Follow your heart and we will be there to aid you."

The Voice had gone, and I was so full of love that I felt as if I were floating far above myself. I could see the chair where my body was sitting a million miles below me, and a rope gently floated down to that place from where I now was.

This was not my first out-of-body experience, but it was the first time I had seen the cord that connected me and my consciousness to my physical body so far below.

I have no idea how much time passed; time had no importance. The rigors of life were non-existent. I was being cradled in the arms of some giant parent, and cuddled in a nurturing way.

I began to make my travel plans later that day and was
stunned to find out that Maria, my travel agent, was a student
of metaphysics and was originally from Peru. I was discovering that there are no accidents in life.

I would be gone a month: two weeks in Mexico and two
weeks in Peru. I would also be returning to the yacatas at
Tsntsunsan and visiting my friends Terí and Raul in Mexico
City.

I had invited Linda to again go with me to Mexico and
Peru, but she said that this time it was better for me to go
alone.

My class was going very well and I was getting instruction
from the Voice. There were seven women in the class, and we
were creating a very safe place with loving energy for me to
teach in. This energy was also conducive for the students to
learn how to channel, which was what I was teaching them. I
would show the women how to make dream logs and interpret
what their higher selves were saying to them, or how to do
meditation exercises for opening the third eye.

I never knew until the afternoon of the class what I would
be teaching; only at that point would I be told by the Voice
what it was that I should teach. Each lesson was always
something that I had innately known to do in order to teach
myself. It could have been gazing into a crystal or a bowl of
water without blinking for half an hour or more, or it could
have been psychometrizing rocks or other little objects wrapped in tissue paper. When I wrapped objects in tissue paper,
the students couldn't get impressions from their analytical
minds, and instead had to get their feelings from the objects.
Many times they were very clear, and got mental pictures from
the area of the world where I had bought the objects. It was
like a psychic aerobics class intended to hone the senses.

I always ended each class with twenty or so psychic impressions for each person, or else the Voice would come
through with a short lesson on something universal. We all
learned a lot from those early classes about the "bioplasmic
universe" and how energy and information were available to
us all. We were taught to see spirit, understand ectoplasm, use

energy, and much more. It was elevating and it felt good. We all experienced the feeling that we had the ability to expand and be connected to the Source.

Several times during class we experienced some strange occurrences. Once a lamp turned itself on when the Voice started to speak, and turned itself off when the Voice finished. The class was floored. I tried to be as calm as possible, and just explained that all things were possible when we place our belief in the Creator.

About a month before I was set to go on my journey, during one of my classes, a face appeared on the lace curtains. It was quite large, and floated an inch or two in front of the curtains. It spoke to me and I repeated the words:

"We are pleased with your progress. In five minutes we will show ourselves in the southwest quadrant of the sky, directly over your house. This is the physical proof that we are here, and that our love for you is present at all times."

I started explaining the power of spirit to the class: "When one is open to new ideas and doesn't demand proof, it is often presented. If one is critical, skeptical or scoffing, there is no receiving and hence no proof is given."

The entire class moved outdoors, and saw the manifestation of a saucer over the top of my house. It appeared as a spectacular blue-white light with blue, green, and red beams emanating from its center in no particular pattern, unlike a plane. It was as if the ship were a ball of light with starbeams of color piercing the night.

The ship made a very slow-moving descent, then zigzagged, abruptly split to the left, and disappeared. This was magic, as far as most of us were concerned. It was a miracle. It was real, and yet it left us with the feeling that time had passed us by. There was no time, no space, just an infinite expanse of universe, and we were one of the stars.

Midnight blue seemed to envelop me, and I stood there alone in front of the house, in another world that was truly a miracle of creation. All the history which had gone before had vanished. Those thousands of souls who had watched the skies before me must have felt this, too. A golden beam of light seemed to emerge from my heart and flow through the cosmos, sending my love for the world in every direction. I was whole and free to be just another being in a master plan, who had chosen to live and love in harmony with my fellow people.

It was as if I were riding a wave which would never crash to the shore, because the shore didn't exist for me. There were no secrets in the universe. All of the mysteries dwelt within me, and I was being beckoned to follow that golden beam to discover the cosmos within my own consciousness.

I was out of my body and the Voice seemed to be whispering in my left ear, but my left ear was light years from where I floated in this beautiful maze of stars. I was total perception. I was able to see in all directions. I was both hearing and feeling textures, and music was playing inside my heart. Such joy was amazing!

The Voice began to speak:

"You are a creative force in the universe. You are whole. The light you create can allow you to be a source of love and comfort to others, but you must trust yourself and the light within you. These lessons will be yours to choose for yourself. There is no failure in the universe. All things continue and will evolve. The foremost law of All That Is is that each being will continue to evolve at its own rate. There are no boundaries or stops unless they are self-created. All emotions are chosen and created by you for you to experience. All emotions, actions, and reactions are a source of lessons that each source must experience for itself. Find that path in love. We will support your every decision, for each one will allow you to grow."

I was still in an altered state of consciousness when we returned to the house. It was so difficult for me to speak at that moment that I ended the class and sent the students on their way.

I was in dreamland the instant my head hit the pillow. I returned to that place within my consciousness where I became the universe, undivided by my own considerations and doubts, and I began to make my decisions. I decided that I really was here for a purpose, and that I was to challenge myself to walk on that path for growth. My trip to Peru would be a major lesson to see if I had really understood the Voice and the lessons of life and love and evolution that I had received.

"Exaltation is the going of an inland soul to sea . . ."
Emily Dickinson

— *Ten* —

July sweltered in Los Angeles as I packed for the cool weather of Mexico's rainy season and the winter in the Peruvian highlands. I realized that the trip back to Mexico was really a chance to review all the feelings I had experienced before. I needed to examine my feelings of mistrust in myself, and what I had experienced during the last trip. I had to laugh at myself in between the long underwear and the cosmetics.

I was on the road again — another adventure, and I still felt that nobody would understand. Who would believe that a girl from Waco, Texas was going to Peru to meet extraterrestrials? It seemed like this had all started a thousand years ago, yet only nine months had passed.

As I placed item after item in the suitcase, I was already seeing what I wanted to accomplish during the upcoming adventure. I remembered how dangerous that had been on the last trip. Preconceived ideas sure do keep you from relaxing into an experience as it happens! I felt as though I could stop that process from happening this time, so I just laughed at it and decided to stay in the moment. Each moment would present itself in its own time, and I would be able to learn and enjoy these moments as they came.

Tomorrow was the big day, and I was restless. I woke to the sound of the Voice telling me what I needed to know.

"Now you are ready, little one. There are three doorways to space. One is in your Bermuda Triangle, one twenty miles due north of the north pole, and the last at Machu Picchu. You will be exposed to energies from the fourth dimension that will activate physical changes within your body. This will be an adjustment period so that you can handle the energies from higher levels of consciousness. Stay aware. The excess of higher vibrations could create a physical problem. Do what you feel is right for you and all will be okay."

I was stunned by the information. I had caught a sizeable

cold on the last trip from an excess of psychic energy which
had blown out several electrical items near me, and that was
just from energy produced by the pyramids! This time it was
going to be "black hole energy." I had heard about it from
Seth, an entity channeled by Tom Massari, a few weeks earlier.
Tom had been channeling Seth for a couple of years, and I
had gone to see him three times for private sessions. Seth had
been very helpful to me in my times of doubt, when I needed
assurance. However, I wanted to know more, so I decided to
ask the Voice.

"Is the energy you are talking about 'black hole energy?'"

*"Yes, it is a channel, if you choose to call it that, where energies
converge and are assimilated into your three-dimensional physical
world. The laws within this space are unknown by your peers and
many have gone in and never returned to your dimension. The
energies within this space are governed by no rules or laws. They are
governed only by the perceptions and decisions of the beings using
the space. Total concentration and one-mindedness is necessary to
stay centered in this space. If one were to become confused, he would
never return, because all directions are equal, all dimensions the
same, and one stray thought would allow the space to be changed
into a different idea of the same thing. This is why many of the ships
and planes which have disappeared in the Bermuda Triangle have
never returned. Too many stray thoughts and panic."*

I was trying to grasp what the Voice was telling me. It was difficult to perceive the wholeness of it. I asked what I believed to
be a simple question, and got a very intense answer.

"What does this have to do with me? I won't get lost in this
space, will I?"

*"No, little one. However, all beings have a similar space in their
brains and consciousness that is used to receive telepathic communication. When this area of the brain or consciousness is open,
information and impressions are free to come in. The information
can be very difficult to handle, and if one's purpose is not clear,
could lead to confusion. Many persons in your society have gone
insane by finding the way to enlightenment without trusting
themselves. When this occurred, they were not ready to handle the
energy and considered it a curse. They believed they were going*

*insane and created the idea of madness. This, in turn, paved the
way to real insanity, and negative thoughts about themselves fed
that energy into the computers they call their brains.*

*"Like creates like. In this way, those persons created their own
hell and confusion. This is the disease known as fear. It, like
everything else, is self-created. You have chosen to treat this experience as an adventure, and therefore are creating it to be a
beautiful experience. Just take your time on this road to discovery.
Our love goes with you."*

I realized that hours had elapsed since the Voice had stopped, and I was looking at the world through different eyes. I
was reviewing all that had happened to me in my life, and
could clearly see how I had allowed outside influences to
direct me and confuse me when I had had difficulty. I was, in
turn, creating more negativity by buying into that almighty
opinion from the other fellow. I truly began to see in its
proper light what I had learned in Sunday School years ago:
that when the Bible said God gave humanity free will, that
meant *free*. We are free to create our own heaven or hell, and
that is "God's will be done." After all, each person is created in
the image of the Creator and given the right of way in all
cases. There are no victims. If we only had that ability to keep
firmly attached to love and light, we would always experience
the magic in life.

How in the world would I ever be able to tell anyone what
I was truly experiencing? Would they have to go through it for
themselves? Of course. I did know that the door could be opened
if they wanted to hear. I began to see that the trip would be tying up a lot of loose ends.

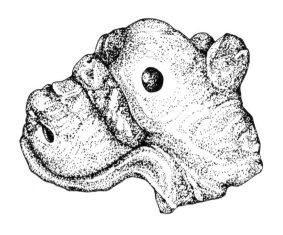

BLUE THUNDER

Blue thunder, night rain,
    with echoes of the pyramids to
      bring me home again.
Within these magic mountains
    a part of me remains
        while the other part goes searching
          for a lover without a name. . .

— *Eleven* —

Terí and Raul were waiting at the plane in Mexico. I was a bundle of nerves and couldn't hold back the tears. It was as if I had lived a thousand lives since I had last seen them. We were planning to take the children and go to Morelia the very next morning for a period of four days. In the meantime, we had hours of non-stop news to catch up on.

I would have one glorious week to visit in Mexico before my Peruvian adventure began. That first evening was Raul's anniversary of twenty years in his own business, and with all their friends around, the subject eventually turned to metaphysics.

When everyone learned that I was going to Peru alone, the women were shocked and the gentlemen curious to see what I planned to do without any companions. I was really surprised to see how brave everyone believed I was.

"Don't you know anyone in Peru?" one woman asked.

"No, but I expect to know a lot of people by the time I leave," I replied.

At that point, the full spectrum of shocked faces was laughable. I began to explain that I was fully competent and that I had the Voice with me. Everyone in Mexico has had some kind of mystical thing or another happen to them, and all it takes is one word from you that you believe in spirits before the stories begin to fly.

I was happy to do a little psychometry and show these new friends what fun it was to see the pictures I could pick up from their keys or rings. Psychometry is the process of holding an object and psychically receiving impressions from it regarding what it is, where it's from, and its history of interactions. From its vibrations, a sensitive can receive psychic pictures or feelings. We took it all lightly, and had lots of laughs at some of the funny things I saw.

The ride to Morelia was beautiful. We took a route very different from the ones I had taken before. In one of the pueblos we passed, there was an old gold mine and several small Catholic churches left from the days of the early Spanish settlements. The gold must have given out, because the town was just a shell. High on one hill was the ruin of what appeared to have been a near-palace. I was fascinated with the long colonnades running along the outside.

Down the tiny winding road towards the next town was a field of the blue maguey plants which produce the finest te-quila in Mexico. They take a long time to grow, and are uprooted and killed to make the brew of the gods. It is the plant of medicine in Mexico. Its leaves can be pounded to make thread or hemp, and the points of the leaves, although they contain poison, can be used for primitive needles. A lit-tle man beside the field caught my attention. His eyes were piercing and his smile was hauntingly familiar. I could have sworn that he was the same wizard I had seen in Pasquero the year before. When I turned my head to see him as we passed, he was gone. Vanishing seemed to be a specialty with him!

As the car continued down the road, I noticed that Raul Jr. and Marianna were sleeping. I must have been put into a light trance state myself, because the wizard invaded my dreams: "You are looking at the illusion of life. You created me in your world so that I could tell you how impermanent the players on the stage can appear. When you dream, you create the next turn your life will take. Your power is yet to be truly yours. Use it well. Don Ignacio has spoken." He had come to me before as a blind beggar, taken my money and vanished, just to teach me a lesson. Now he was just a mirage in my mind. Even without his apprentices, he was awesome.

As he disappeared from my vision, I continued to see strange lands and distorted features. I saw a giant mountain that was hollow, and a landing field, many spacecraft, and tiny beings three-and-a-half feet high. I understood that these other beings could reside anywhere by mentally creating the space, and yet could never be detected because most of us were walking around in a solid, unsuspecting reality. We didn't believe that it could be so. By not allowing the possibility, we had created the most effective and most permanent protection possible for the other beings from our universe.

I was determined to open that door for myself. I wanted to find the answers to life. It was a real struggle to get my eyes open, but we were nearing Morelia so I forced myself back to consciousness.

The Villa Montana was perfect, as usual, and all of us had a wonderful time the first few days. We visited the ruins at Tsntsunsan and romped through the red mud in a nearby field to find obsidian arrowhead-like pieces from days long gone. The vibrations coming from the little pieces of obsidian were tremendous; the power was wonderful. The power of that healing invaded my consciousness; I began to see visions, and the Voice began. The primitive knowledge of how to cut open a skull and relieve the pressure of a body in agony invaded my memory. I saw the writhing body of a young man, and the look of gratitude in his eyes, along with a brief, weak smile, before he closed his eyes. The pulsating pieces of obsidian warmed my hand, sending shocks of energy up my arm.

"Once again, you have discovered your past. The healing of others has been your quest for many lifetimes. As a Mayan healer, you traveled far to show these warlike peoples how to heal and live in peace. The Tolucans of this area were using the power of dark magic to control their enemies.

"With your knowledge of the healing arts, you came as an emissary to shed light into that darkness. The final result was death. Your efforts were stopped by the priest in the temple that has yet to be uncovered. He, Mixcoalcoal, was losing the power to control the masses, and he arranged for you to be given as human sacrifice to the god of rain, Tlaloc. The coming storm was supposed to stop the enemy from advancing."

The vision before me was one of water rising and rain pouring, a volcano in the background erupting, and a serpent-like knife being driven into my heart. I realized that I was standing in mud, here in the twentieth century, and that rain had begun in truth. I couldn't pull my feet from the spot. The sucking sound of the earth made me panic. I was seeing

Linda's dream from a year before, and thought that I was to be destroyed here again.

The entirety of the situation suddenly frightened me as the rain began beating at me. I frantically looked around. Marianna and the tiny boy from the village were nowhere in sight. Little Pedro had vanished with Marianna, behind the mule corn, to find other pieces of obsidian. I fought to rid myself of the knee- deep, rust-colored mud. My right leg came loose, but my shoe was sliding off a foot below the mud. I curled my toes and pulled, determined not to allow myself the luxury of screaming.

I began to relive my fight in that other lifetime with Mix-coalcoal, knowing that somewhere beneath this ooze his bones and blackened soul wanted me again. He was losing his power because I was healing his victims with love, helping them to rid themselves of fear, yet here I was fearing the situation, causing his power to increase. Because I was not centered, it fed energy to the memory of him. Ideas are given power by the thinker. The implosion of his dark, volcanic mind was still holding this power. He had never moved to the light. Unwilling to give up his lust for control, he was here, trying once again to bring others into slavery. Was he still commanding the rain and wind in his black, blood-caked robes? Was he here with me now, wanting to take me to the darkness below to stop my search for truth?

The Voice came to me, saying, *"There is no control unless you give it your power. That power is your fear of it. Slavery of souls is by their agreement. No one can control another person except by feeding and nurturing their fear."*

Suddenly, my feet were free. I stood looking at how my own doubt and fear had fed the energy of that benign mud. The impotence of a situation which had one moment ago seemed life-threatening was now laughable. I giggled as I tromped through the field and climbed the stone walls to get back to the ruins. I was not going to say a word to Raul or Terí. I had learned my lesson, and that was enough.

That night, after dinner, I went to my room high above the Villa and lit a fire. From my bed, I watched the flames dance across the tiled floor and play with the patterns of the hand-woven woolen rugs. The old Spanish colonial cabinet, with its rich dark wood, glimmered in the light of the kerosene lamp, and I felt at home in my heart.

Through hand-woven cotton curtains, slightly open on the north window, I peeked at the night sky. Clouds were gathered, and the lightning began. Watching the impending autumn storm, I heard a song within me, rising with the call of the wilderness beyond my cozy room.

The song was in a language I had long forgotten, a language from another time, when I had been a Native American. The memory was vague, but was becoming stronger as I allowed the words to slip from my lips. "Hye nah oka nay, Hye nah oka nay," the song was seeking wholeness in my vision quest, searching for the goddess energy within each being: wholeness that was thought to be found in a mate. The irony of my quest was that wholeness was only to be found within oneself. The goddess energy is the female receptive energy within all creation that allows men and women to receive divine energy. The source of creation is Adonai, The Ever-Living One, which we call God. I began to see that this Creator was both male and female in energy, and that the energy was love. This love manifested itself in the form of light. Male, positive energy was the part of each being that thrusted forward and searched for experience in creation. The goddess energy — female, receptive energy — was the part of each being that made the turn to face the experience of creation and received the streamings of love and light from the Creator, using the emotion of male experience to seek the truths within.

"The willingness to seek one's source and to heal one's body, mind, and spirit comes from the goddess energy. The male, positive energy is the portion of each being that is mental, analytical, and identity-oriented," said the Voice. *"The ultimate test of the spiritual warrior is in relinquishing control. This control is the desire to be 'the cause' in all life situations, rather than 'the effect.' This is an ambiguity, in that it is the false glimmering of power or beingness. The power lies in the harmony or willingness to ex-*

perience all life functions with the same degree of love and understanding."

I asked the Voice what it meant by relinquishing control. It sounded to me as if one should become a victim of life or that one should become a follower, in a sense.

"No, little one. The power lies in understanding that you are creating every act in your life to enhance your growth. The life-lessons are learned by not fighting the acts you create, but in learning from them. When control is relinquished, these lessons become a way of self-expression. The song you were chanting has a vibratory rate that was a part of your vision quest in that other life when you were a plains Indian. This set of tones will allow you to revisit your past and to see the lessons you learned then."

The chant grew louder in my mind, and I allowed it to flow from my lips as I relinquished control to the goddess energy within. The room turned misty and I stared into the flames. The lightning and thunder became a part of me, and my spirit was at one with the wind.

I was looking at a marriage ceremony on an open plain. My husband-to-be looked into my eyes, and I realized that we were dressed in ceremonial buckskins. The intricate beading on my bodice told the secrets of my total being. In front of us was fire, and medicine shields that relayed, through art, our separate spiritual lives and quests for unity with the Great Spirit.

The shields were planted on spears, mine on his side facing him, and his on mine facing me. The mystery of my shield was to be spoken to him, then his to me.

My lips parted and the words filled my heart as they spilled forth. "I am Midnight Song, a dreamer of dreams. In innocence I come to you from the south. My shield is the midnight sky, star-filled with the quarter moon. I am a rainbow woman and artist, a seer and healer of pain. I am quick to follow the clouds and forget my duty as a wife. I am true to the Grandfathers and will give you my love from the deepest spring that flows within me that we may grow old together. I ask that you dream with me and allow me to follow in your understanding."

My husband-to-be smiled; his eyes were the kindness I had been longing for. The passion kindled in that moment was awesome to experience in his silent form. He bore his soul with his words.

"I am Dreamwalker, a shaman of visions and cures. In wisdom I come to you from the north. My shield is the white stallion dancing in the purple dream rain. I am a rainbow man and seer who will guard your innocent way as you climb the sacred mountain, seeking wholeness. Your way must be your own, but I will honor the climb and bless the Mother Earth for cradling you in her breast as you grow old with me."

The ceremony was completed as we jumped the fire together. Feasting continued until all was quiet and we were alone together in the wedding lodge. A woman covered the tepee door with crossed spears, and our shields hung together as one.

I felt words trying to come from my lips, and grabbed a pen and paper as they formed in my mind. The vision persisted as I spoke this poem to Dreamwalker, there in our first moments of intimacy:

WEDDING SONG

Sing to me, my husband, of days long gone.
Of nights beneath a melon moon with
Firelight flickering gently and
Love's reflections on the tepee walls.

And I will sing to you, Dreamwalker,
Of sun-filled mornings, the call of doves.
My heart awakening within the protection
Of your strong arms; greeting the day.

And together we will remember the songs
Of those that rode the wind before us,
As they made their way; gathering the goodness

Of the earth and returning their love to the land.
For we are all that ever has been and
All that ever will be. . .
Reflections of the quest for life or
The spirit within the breeze.

And to that end, our lives are blessed
For we will always be. . .
a part of the Force
that forever exists. . .
Within infinity.

    I put the notebook down and walked to the window. The vision was gone. Such love filled me that tears spilled wantonly from my eyes. There was no shame or regret in these tears, and as I peered into the window it was difficult to distinguish, there upon the pane, whether it was tears I saw, or rain.

CHILD WITHIN

Teach me how to touch the stars,
  To give the sky a smile,
    To wait for the rainbow after the storm.
And I will give you
  the laughter of my eyes,
    The warmness of my love,
And the one thing that no one else has been able to touch:

  The little girl
    that grew up inside this heart of mine.

— *Twelve* —

The next day in Morelia was filled with tennis and swimming for Teri, Raul, and the children. I was an observer. As my thoughts wandered to the night before, I longed for the privacy of my mountaintop room, the coolness of the azure evening, and my pinewood fire.

The after-dinner quiet filled with pensive guitar music as I bid everyone goodnight. I stole away to my room, high above the guests gathering for coffee and liquors in the salon. Sleep seemed unattainable as I rode waves of memory into the experience of the night before. It was drizzling, and the fire brought me such loving warmth that I slipped into a dreamlike state without noticing it.

The Voice was calling me. In front of the fire, I saw images of many lives pass before me, becoming the flames, dancing up the chimney into vanishing sparks. It didn't even seem funny to me that I could see through the back wall of the chimney. The sky was translucent indigo, and a golden glow from Venus filtered through the clouds into my room.

The Voice began as a whisper, but as I tuned into the channel to hear it better, the energy rose and the Voice gained clarity.

"You have viewed many of your physical lifetimes, and now it is time to see the overview. Upon entry into the third dimension or density, you become a primary soul with your first physical form. It was at this time that the wheel of experience or karma began."

"But what happened before that? Was I just a thought?"

"In a sense, the first dimension and second dimension were experienced as thought-forms; however, we of the Council of Light prefer to call them consciousness units. In every atom, there are units of consciousness: male, female, and divine. In first density, it is

experiencing the elements of air, earth, water, and fire. In the second density, it is experiencing plant and animal, insect and cellular forms."

"Are you telling me that I might have been an animal or insect?"

"No, but as a unit of consciousness, all atoms are connected and all thoughts and ideas travel through the whole."

"Oh, then I was just gaining knowledge of creation through viewing the whole?"

The Voice paused and then continued: *Before you were a primary soul, you were a cell in the body of another human being, gaining the knowledge of teamwork in running a physical body. This is one reason that it is important to love your body. There are approximately thirty trillion units of consciousness in your body that may choose to finish their life lessons in second density and become primary souls in third density."*

I was in awe, and as I was trying to sort out the magnitude of what had been expressed, lightning cracked and thunder rattled the entire building. The lights went out.

"Does this mean that we are killing souls when we split the atom with the bombs that have been created by our scientists?"

The sadness of the Voice created sudden stinging tears in my eyes, and a lump like an ostrich egg in my throat.

"Yes, little one. . .The destructiveness of your race has long been a deep sadness to us. The lack of love is devastating to behold, for it is carried by atoms and the seven spiralling energy threads in each, to every other atom in all of creation."

"Are you telling me that every action and thought in the universe is available to every living thing?"

"Yes, and those beings of higher awareness can and do view the shock waves of anger and destruction with love and compassion. We feel sadness in the viewing but are also understanding of the process. All experience simply is. In being, souls must experience the Law of Confusion to distinguish what is correct for them. If they choose to serve themselves and their ego out of self-love, that is one polarity. The other polarity is service to others. In choosing service to others, one is serving the whole of creation and therefore serving self as an equal part of the whole."

"Then you are saying that each of us has free choice to live the way we wish."

"There is always free will — it is a natural law. It is the way in which a being gains experience and the way in which each being finds or denies its connection to the Creator."

"Well, if that is the process, how do we continue to evolve past the physical stage?"

"As you know, there are non-physical lifetimes in your third density. These are on another level within the third dimension. They are the times one views life and the lessons just experienced in truth and with free will. If the being is striving toward a service-to-self pattern, it will choose lessons that will aid it in experiencing the other side of any wrongs it feels it has previously inflicted on another. Other times, the being will choose to aid a fellow soul by being a worthy opponent in that person's life."

"What do you mean by a worthy opponent? Is it someone that fights with you or kills you?"

"It can be. But in the usual sense, it is a being who will present to another soul the one thing that the other soul needs to learn about itself. It is not always pleasant. It is also usually a two-way street."

"Oh, you mean like my relationship with my little sister when I was growing up. She was homecoming queen, cheerleader, and most popular girl in her class. I was not interested in these things, but I was jealous."

"Yes, but if you remember after her second child was born, she confided that she had told lies to your parents to get you in trouble because of her jealousy of you."

I thought about what the Voice had said before replying.

"So you are saying that when we worked out our differences, and Donna saw how much I loved her, that I was no longer a worthy opponent to her. All those lonely years in which she had tried to hurt me were actually a way to teach me how to love myself. . .even if I wasn't homecoming queen and all that?"

"That is the gist of the situation, but there are many more subtleties. Both were competing for the love of their parents, one through achievement in school and thoughtful actions, and you

through rebellion and attention-seeking through the drama of loneliness. Both were equal attempts to seek approval of self from parents. Both were fighting the reflection of another part of yourselves. The polarity was introversion and extroversion, showing both sides in each of you."

The puzzle was coming together for me, and I felt a new respect for the chosen pathways of others. I was seeing life from a new perspective. The dawning of understanding was filling me with compassion for all of my fellow beings, and I was content just to muse about this for a few minutes. I was realizing that all lessons in life are perfect, even if some are uncomfortable. I had learned compassion and love from the ones I considered the hardest.

The fire had reduced itself to glowing orange embers laced with purple hues. I plopped on another log and walked to the bathroom. I needed a break, and the fresh, cool mountain water gave my face a titillating rebirth. Grabbing my long, soft flannel nightgown, I quickly changed, then patted my face dry.

Catching my reflection in the mirror, I was amazed that I looked the same. There was the same thick, long brown hair, the same pale skin, and even the same eyes. I moved closer to the mirror and looked deep into my own eyes.

When I was nine, I had seen craters in those hazel eyes. They had reminded me of some long-forgotten place that I was no longer a part of. The clear green of my irises was surrounded by a grey-brown which, closer to the center, faded to amber before disappearing into the black pupils. In the green portion, the color would change to grey or blue-green with my moods, but the ocean-like craters always remained.

The eyes are said to be the windows of the soul. Do they change from lifetime to lifetime? I was seeing worlds of a different ilk in my own eyes now. Was it the Voice's words which had set these new worlds free? Flower petals were opening in the craters of my eyes, and from each flower another one began to bloom.

Creation of life is constant, never static. Realizing that you are a part of that creation, and allowing yourself to bloom, is the key.

Would anyone see the change in my inner being, or would the private storm continue to rage in my soul? Would I have to continue to judge myself by what others could see, or could I finally be at one with the self I was becoming? It was the self I had always been afraid to be.

REBIRTH

After the rain,
    the oil on the pavement painted phantom faces,
        and shapes that seemed to beckon me out of doors.
The wind was chilly for summer,
    the last trace of thunder rolled by me,
        helping to clear the sky.
The freshness of the air was a sign
    that the earth had been refreshed.
        And today was another day. . .
           not like yesterday
              or totally unlike tomorrow. . .
But a new beginning for the parched earth
        and me.

— *Thirteen* —

I walked to the door and opened the brass latch. The sounds below had evaporated. I stepped out on the tile terrace and gazed down at the sleeping city of Morelia.

The night air chilled my face, and I shuddered involuntarily when the wind caressed my body. The thunderclouds had parted; above me, the night sky had borne stars.

The terrace was scattered with stone carvings of elephants, fish, burros, and saints. Knowing Mexican history as I did, the combination didn't seem incongruous. The earlier religions had been based on nature and its forces, and each animal had been a potential ally or deity. When the Spaniards came, the pyramids and temples of these nature religions had been defaced, and Catholic cathedrals had been built over their former power places.

One could find God in all things. There was no need to destroy another person's idea of God just to feed one's own need to be right. I began musing about the order of the universe and the Creator as I slipped back into the bungalow.

With a glass of iced tea, I headed for the stretched-pigskin chair by the blazing fire. The rhythm of the flames soon lulled me into a receptive space, and the Voice invaded my privacy once more.

"After achieving the lessons of many lifetimes on the physical plane, one chooses to be harvested into fourth density."

"Wait a minute, what is being 'harvested'?"

The souls that have completed third density are eligible, by virtue of their desire to continue to evolve, to move into fourth density. Harvesting is just that. Many are transformed at the same moment. It occurs about every 25,000 years."

"Oh, you said that we 'choose' to be harvested. What if someone doesn't choose to be harvested?"

"If the being does not have the urge to evolve, it is not truly

ready for harvest. The natural law of free will always applies."

"Well, does that mean if you're good you'll go to heaven?"
I giggled.

"All beings of the 'service-to-others' mode and all beings of the 'service-to-self' mode are harvested equally."

"Are you saying that bad people go on to fourth density, too?!"

"Little one, you are judging. All beings are equally creating from love."

"But how can that be? The people who hurt others are living for themselves. Why do they get to move on like the ones who helped others through love?"

"The beings that choose the path of service to self are acting from supreme love for themselves and no love for others. That is a separate fourth density. That portion consists of all of the beings of service to self."

"Are you saying that after this physical part of evolution the beings of love and light are separated from those that have chosen to live for themselves alone?"

"Yes, child, that is so. It is in the third density physical realm that each being makes the choice. Those that choose service to others become aware that when they serve others they are serving the whole of creation. In serving all, *they are serving the Creator through serving every other living thing — thereby serving themselves, for all living things are a part of each of us. We are all cells in the body of the I AM."*

The intensity of the communication made my head reel. I struggled to grasp it all. It was nearly dawn and my body ached from being in the same position for so long. Painfully stretching my stiff limbs, I shuffled to bed. The white starched sheets felt heavenly as I pulled the covers over me, sliding into dream-filled bliss.

When dawn crept in the window, I bolted upright. "That was no dream!" I thought. "No dream could be that real!" During the night a woman had come to me in a dream. She was the same lady who had appeared to me when I was nine years old. At that time, I had heard my father scream, "Who are you? What do you want? Are you an angel? I'm not ready to die! Get out of here! Get out of here!"

A golden glow had appeared on my bedroom wall, and I had seen a beautiful lady standing at the foot of my bed. She glowed a tawny shade of yellow, and had bright blue, oriental eyes. Her body was translucent, and the cloth shimmering around her looked like the iridescence of dragonfly wings.

She had spoken to me, saying that my father did not understand why she had come. She had told me that the years ahead would be difficult for me, but that I was here for a purpose. She then promised to return when I was ready to take my place in the world. Finally she kissed my forehead and vanished. Even today, my forehead bears a tiny, round indentation where she kissed my third eye.

Daddy had told the story of his fright and fury when she had appeared; I held my one and only secret to myself. His friends had thought his tale curious, since he had been awake when it happened, but I knew that it had been something special.

The realization was slow in taking hold, but tonight I became convinced that this beautiful lady was my Voice. During the night, in my altered state, I had seen her once again. She hadn't told me her name, but she had reminded me that we had been together many times before, and that she was still nurturing my spiritual growth.

I emerged from my reverie, a bell clanging in the court-yard reminding me that Terí, Raul, and the children would be waiting for me in the dining room if I didn't hop to it and get dressed. Today, our last day in Morelia, I just wanted to be alone and absorb everything I had experienced. I felt obligated to go wherever Raul and Terí wanted to go, but my heart tore me the other way — solitude was my first choice.

As luck would have it, the children told us they didn't want to go to the zoo or the city — they had made friends with some new children. The adults decided to make a quick trip to town for a look at the market, and then go back to the Villa for the rest of the day.

After lunch, I headed for a much-needed siesta. Once again, I was visited by my luminous friend — but it was more like a vision than a dream, since I wasn't yet asleep. She told me to try to remember a dream I had had the year before in which I had used the phrase "estan borrados." I had no trouble recalling this dream, since I had never used the phrase myself and had had to look it up in my Spanish dictionary. It translated as "they have vanished or erased." In the dream, I had been looking for something, and I had yelled up to my friends on the balcony above, "Están borrados!" In the months since the dream, I had wondered about its significance.

"That dream was a spiritual quest for you, little one. You had been looking for the clues to your past, and they had vanished. Now that you are truly seeking, all will be made available. Rest and refresh yourself, for this evening we will continue your education. You already know the answers. This is just the relearning that every being experiences when it makes the connection to the total or higher self."

I seemed to remember mumbling a thank-you before totally dissolving into sleep.

That evening I was anxious to finish dinner and meditate, but the evening was full of old friends, music, and fond farewells. It was close to midnight when I climbed the tile steps to the room that had become my sanctuary amid the bright Mexican stars. The scent of night-blooming jasmine made my senses jump, and then I realized — there was no jasmine here! A copper pot of carnations stood on the table, but no jasmine.

For years I had smelled jasmine when there had been none in the vicinity, always accompanied by a sense of well-being and security. I now realized that this was the key. It was *her* scent, the lady of light who had been with me all these years. So she had been waiting for me!

Quickly, I built a fire and peeled off my clothes. My nightgown was soft and fluffy sliding across my legs. Propping a pillow on the rug, I sat before the flames, straightening my back and calming my internal chatter. The vast waves of excitement which filled me were not helping me achieve the serene state that I was aiming for. I breathed deeply, and released the breath. A sudden weightlessness made it feel as if all the energy in and around me were altering at once, with no degree of subtlety. This happened instantaneously, and the environment of my sanctuary suddenly vanished.

The world opened, and I bloomed with it. My lady of light began speaking almost immediately.

"As each being evolves in its own unique way, the paths will be different and yet the same. The adventure lies within the creativity of each soul. Be at one with the energy and follow the path in love. Relax yourself and know that you have created this opportunity for yourself because the time is right."

"All right, I'm ready. I feel like a newborn child. I want to see all of this glorious creation that you call All That Is."

"That takes many millennia, my child. The overview is all that you need at present so that you can reach for the future. The urge toward that end is within you now and will be a light to your path. We can only assist that 'seeking' if you desire the information."

"Oh yes, I want to know. I've always had a million questions about where we go and what we do after these physical lives."

"After the physical third-density lives, you have a series of densities containing beings of light that learn the lessons of service to others. Unconditional love is learned in the fourth density, as well as telepathic thought. In this way, beings learn how all things have consciousness and can be communicated with."

"What is a 'light being,' exactly?"

"Do you remember when I appeared to you when you were a child, and again in your office?"

"Yes, of course. You were glowing."

"That is because the atoms of higher densities are very rapid, and therefore not as solid. The consciousness units within the atoms are in harmony with the vibration of my purpose and connection to All That Is. The subatomic particles are mirrors that reflect the love from The Ever-Living One as I allow myself to be used as an instrument of that love."

"Are you saying that when someone comes into harmony with the Source, there is no more negativity within them?"

"In a sense. There are no more particles of what you call ego or personality. . .those ideas called ego are the reason that pure love

cannot flow through any being. The need for identity."

"Do you not have a name, then?"

"Yes, I have had many names, but they are only fragments of the whole. I am a humble servant of the light and that is all you need for right now. My name will not be of any importance to you. Later, if it is needed, we will send it to you telepathically."

"Are these needs for identity the reason why we cannot seem to live together in peace as a total group of people?"

"Yes, my child, the ego is the reflection of a need to serve one's own needs and one's own sense of importance. You physical beings are going through the process of decision and life lessons so you can see that all life is equal. Those that do not see it are simply seeing identity as a means to achieve what they believe is power. The true power comes from reflecting the love of the Creator and being that love.

"Well, what comes after learning that reflected love?"

"That is All That Is. It is expressed through the one hundred major levels of consciousness in spiritual evolution. They are called densities. Each density has thousands of lessons, as there are as many unique ways to learn as there are beings in this universe. After the seventh density, beings that had light bodies become pure thought and are then given lessons in how to manifest those ideas in the form you call physical."

"What do you mean? What kind of things do they manifest?"

"The manifestations are what you call creation. The love and light that is reflected by these beings from eighth to approximately thirtieth density are ideas of beauty, like in the cosmos when you look at the night sky, or the beginning of a new planet in a new solar system. From thirtieth to sixtieth density, the being will be the spiritual consciousness of that fully manifested planet."

"Wait a minute! I will someday be a planet?"

"Yes, and your lessons then will have to do with allowing beings to inhabit your surface and to use your resources to enable them to experience the physical lives you will be enacting."

"This is really heavy. I'm having a hard time with these concepts. Why do we become planets?"

"Every being learns to manifest a planet so that the love from

the sun in that solar system can reflect as a division of the Source, its reflected portion of All That Is."

"Are you saying that we will become suns or stars, too?"

"Yes. From around sixtieth to ninety-fifth density, each being becomes a larger reflection of the Creator's love."

"Hold on a minute! I'm really getting blown away! I want to understand, but this is really a lot to handle. How do we become suns or stars?"

"Little one, this is done when the capacity for divine love that any being can handle is expanded. The source is constantly and forever creating love, and it is given to those that expand their capacities to handle and reflect that love."

"Then the more we grow toward the idea of total love, the more love we are given."

"No. All beings are given the same amount of this light and love. It is when they choose to accept it and reflect it to others that their capacity is multiplied."

I sighed, then asked, "The more a being gives or reflects pure love, then the more is received to be given, right?"

"That's correct; that is why I was sent to you. Your longings for answers from your first years, along with your giving nature, made it possible for me to serve you. Now it is your choice to serve others and therefore the whole."

The lump in my throat was the size of a golf ball, and stinging tears blurred my vision. I felt so inadequate, so small. I was sobbing, and all the years of loneliness and "feeling different" seemed to be washing away. Oh, the enormity of it all. I needed to be fulfilled. This was it, and there were no boundaries left to stop the flow. It was as if the whole of all those years before were dissolving into a pool of eternal nothingness. The past just vanished. No more personal history existed.

I was needed. My talents, my gifts, could be used. It had been a long road, but I was coming to a new beginning, and this was just a taste of the joy that could be. I got up and washed my face in cold water and returned to the fireplace.

The embers were almost gone and, afraid to pour on more kerosene, I just sat there wondering if I should get a blanket. The Voice returned.

"You are healing yourself, little one. That is the key to unconditional love. Judgment has no place in the continuity of love. Do not judge yourself or others, for one day each and every being will evolve into a total universe and will be the Creator of its own universe. All must learn the lessons of undivided wholeness and unconditional love. Rejoice in that knowledge, and create your lessons well."

LEAH

The urgency of needing to be fulfilled
    streams from my being.
There is nothing left to contain this love.
    It knows no boundaries,
        has no stops,
            waits not on time to make it right.

It will survive,
    beyond my confusion,
        above my fear.
            And it will grow and envelop the two of us.
For that is why you were sent to me.
    And I will fight all the demons
        of galaxies far beyond ours,
            for the right to join you
                in your quest for life. . .

For you are *life* itself,
    and I bathe in the glory
        Of living you
            hour by hour.

— Fourteen —

The old Hotel Bolívar was a delight as I curled up in my bed after what had seemed like an endless flight. I was totally worn out, and the grey Lima sky was not appealing. I had been disappointed at the sad faces and lack of warmth I had observed in the airport and hotel lobby. It was ten in the morning, so I ordered a hot chocolate and waited for room service, making hurried mental notes on what I needed to do tomorrow. I was traveling to Cusco, and would be there and in Machu Picchu for two weeks before returning to Lima and then flying directly to Mexico City again.

The hot chocolate arrived, and I jumped back in bed, sipping the warm brew of grated chocolate and hot milk. It had been a wonderful goodbye at the airport in Mexico with Terí and Raul. I had felt terrible about the midnight flight and their insistence on taking me to the airport. To make up for it, there were lots of alpaca sweaters I wanted to buy for the whole family, and I was busily writing down the sizes when I fell asleep.

I woke to darkness. City sounds wafted through the closed windows and I was hungry. As I thought it would be a good idea to go to dinner, I called the front desk to ask the time. It was five a.m.! I had slept for thirteen hours! I called room service for a roll and some hot tea before calling a taxi to take me to the airport.

I had forgotten how awful it was to have lots of luggage in certain foreign countries. The airport was filled to capacity. It was the height of the tourist season, and Europeans swarmed into the ticket lines. Three hours later, the plane took off.

It was only an hour's flight, but what an incredible flight! Even after breaking through the upper cloud layer, I could still see the high Andean peaks. The German boy next to me asked me to take a few pictures of him. It was a real job — his

35mm camera had a six-inch lens, and I nearly scratched the window, not to mention what happened to my eye. I bumped it and nearly gave myself a shiner!

Cusco was crazy, and there were no empty hotel rooms in the entire town. Thank goodness that Maria, my travel agent, had secured reservations for me. Parts of my hotel had been an old Spanish colonial palace for some long-lost viceroy. The dining room was charming. An open patio and fountain in the center courtyard were visible from the gallery and bar windows.

In the lobby, a new group of arriving guests was supplied with complimentary coca tea to open their lungs. The altitude had already taken its toll on some; others felt nauseous. I took a tour to some of the nearby ruins that afternoon, and was sick myself by the time we returned. The tour was very educational, but tiring.

The concierge recommended that I sleep until my body could handle the lack of oxygen. I hobbled across the tiny cobblestone street to a shop and bought a sweater to wear the next day.

Back in my room, all I could see was visions of the llamas and the tiny women who guided them at the ruins. The quadrangle stones which comprised the walls of the ruins began to swim before me. I psychically saw the unity of the Inca nation crumble under the brass-armored foot of a Spanish conquistador. The foot was as large as the whole expanse of the ruins I had visited hours ago, and it ran red with Inca blood.

Something inside me was screaming, "How could you, how could you do it!" I knew that the Incas had been totally peaceful. They had believed in equality, and all of the subjects had been given land as their families and needs grew. The greed of the Spaniards had ruined it all — in the search for gold and glory. What a pathetic reason to destroy a peaceful empire! So it had been in our world for centuries. I just wanted to sleep. Don't think about it, I told myself.

The next day, the entire hotel staff trickled by to see me in the dining room. I guessed that word had spread fast that I was a psychic. That information was on my visa, and visas had to be shown at the desk since the government owns all hotels in Peru.

I gave fifty or so spot readings, about fifteen minutes of quick impressions, and allowed myself a little time to go shopping and walk around town. When I returned late that afternoon, the concierge met me in the lobby.

"Hi, I'm Caesar Tejeira. My father is a professor here in the University, and is the head of the parapsychology society here in Cusco. If you would like, I could arrange a meeting for the two of you."

"Oh, Caesar, I'd love it. Could you ask your father if I could have him as my guest for lunch tomorrow?"

"Of course. I'm sure you would have a wonderful time together. He speaks only Spanish, but I see that will be no problem for you."

"I'm really thrilled. I will be looking forward to it. Shall we say tomorrow at one-thirty?"

"That will be perfect, as he teaches a class until one."

I was dancing on air. How perfect! There really were no accidents in life. Señor Oscar Tejeira was going to be a real help in finding what I needed to know. I was sure of it. Who better than a native Peruvian to help me find some of the answers to my quest? I was sure he knew about the Nazca plains and giant markings too.

Later that evening, I received Oscar's call. We were to meet in the dining room and get acquainted.

The next day, it seemed like forever until one-thirty. I was nervous, because I wasn't sure what to expect. I had met Ph.D.s who were very stuffy, and I wanted to talk with Oscar honestly, without worrying about what he would think, and without having to tailor or censor my speech.

Oscar was right on time, and we were given the most private table in the dining room. The staff all knew the professor, and lunch was delightful. After the usual small talk, we got down to business. Oscar belonged to a private society founded on Theosophy, a philosophy established by H.P. Blavatsky and based on the historical study of all the occult schools on the planet. Theosophy included a belief in the Great White Brotherhood of Light. Oscar worked with beginning psychics and mediums to help them develop their gifts, and was familiar with groups of metaphysically oriented people around the world. Here in Cusco, most of them found their way to his door to get some history on the Incas or the strange UFO appearances in the area.

"Oscar, I'm here to find something called a 'doorway to space' in Machu Picchu. Not many people know about it, but my guidance has been very specific in instructing me to go there. Have you heard of it?"

"Yes, it has been a long time secret and the ruins are still guarded by the Great White Brotherhood."

"Oh, you mean those books I've read about the Ascended Masters and their secret valley here in Peru somewhere. Do you mean that it isn't a legend? There really is a valley like that?"

"Yes, it is about three days from here, and only the initiated are allowed to enter."

"Have you ever been there?"

"Yes, Jamie, but it was many years ago."

"Okay, but if it's three days from here, how can they guard the ancient secret places they are purportedly guardians of?"

"It is not in the physical that they guard these places. They are spiritual masters who can project themselves to any area. You should know the secret password and hand signal when you enter the ruins here — see, this spot on the map."

Oscar relayed the password and showed me the signal. He then swore me to hold these in secrecy.

"The secrets of initiation will be open to you if you go with a pure heart and an open mind. The force of light will guide you, and I want a full report when you return. Be sure to be back in three days."

Our conversation then turned to many of the groups which came from Europe to see the Nazca plains, and how they overlooked many of the special Inca temples just outside Cusco. Oscar had given a few people tours of these special, out-of-the way places, and was willing to take me when I returned.

I was planning to go to Machu Picchu in two days. The interim time was to be spent in meditation and in setting my plans. Oscar wanted me to spend no more than three days there, but didn't seem to want to tell me why. Though curious about his reasoning, I trusted his loving eyes. It was interesting to watch them crinkle when laughter shook his slender form. His pure olive skin was clear and smooth, even though his hair was almost white. He was sorry that his schedule at the University did not allow him time to accompany me, but he assured me that all would be well. We were to meet again the next day.

It was fascinating to see the polarity between Oscar and his wife. Señora Tejeira was a total vegetarian and a yoga teacher who followed her own spiritual path. I'm sure they each had their own ideas of how to seek wholeness, since he ate meat and smoked cigarettes and she was adamantly against such things for herself. They had been married nearly thirty years and had several grandchildren. I thought it peculiar to see that type of unconditional love, even in Peru where the divorce rate was much lower than in the United States.

Over the next two days, I thought quite a bit about why all these Europeans found it so trendy to come here, and why there were so few Americans. What was it about Americans that kept them from visiting Third World countries? Was it guilt? Did we feel horrible when we saw so much poverty? Or was it just that we were so spoiled that any type of inconvenience left us cold? This beauty shouldn't be missed. The industriousness of these beautiful and colorful souls was incredible to me. They grew their own food, built their own homes from mud and straw, and walked miles every day in the mountains just to earn enough money at market to keep home and life together.

On Sunday, I took a drive to the market in Pisac where all the local artisans gathered, and stopped a few times to take pictures. The Urubamba River was filled with white-water rapids, and the town itself teemed with Europeans. I caught sight of some of the children who were staying at my hotel with their parents. I had played card games with them the previous night in the lobby. We waved, and I was introduced to one of the parents. Their entire group from Lima was on holiday, and was going to visit the ruins in Machu Picchu the same day that I was. They had changed hotels that morning due to the high rates of the peak tourist season. We agreed to meet on the train, since I was traveling alone.

I wandered with my tour-agency guide through the various booths, selecting a few sweaters and lengths of fabric. Then I turned up one aisle and went down a tiny street in the back. There were only ten vendors on this street, their meager wares lying on top of their rebozos. I walked up to one lady to examine some of the ornaments she was selling. They had been made from spoons, which had their original handles replaced by long, pick-like prongs.

The bowl of each spoon was crudely engraved with a rooster. As I admired one, she showed me how to use it to secure a shawl. The shawl was filled with goods, or a baby, and slung over one's back. In front, the two ends of the shawl were crossed, and the ornamental pick was inserted to secure the material. Once they reached the market, the women would use the shawls to lay under their wares. They would etch a circle in the earth, sticking the pick in the center. It was their sundial. The sun let them know when they had to pack up and head for home, lest the dark catch them on some mountain trail far from their adobe huts. Fascinated, I bought three. I decided to walk through the crowd once more before heading to the car.

The cobblestone streets were charming, with two-storied whitewashed buildings jutting out at odd angles. I could peer into little shops run by residents who were trying to bring in a few soles, the money of Peru, to get by.

Rounding a corner, I was nearly knocked to the ground by someone pushing by me on the street. The guide grabbed my arm, helping me keep my balance. I was about to yell at whomever it was but then, looking up, I burst into laughter instead: it had been a three-hundred pound runaway hog! I was stunned, but couldn't ignore the hilarity of the situation. That would be one for the folks back home! Who in Hollywood would believe that you could get run down by a pig in Peru!

Back at the hotel, I was still giggling to myself. I had only a few minutes to clean up before Oscar arrived for that drink we had arranged.

After meeting Oscar in the restaurant, I never did get to tell the pig story. I guess concern about my dignity prevented me from relating it. We had more serious matters to discuss, anyway.

We had been seated near the bar but, annoyed by the noise there, we moved to a corner table across from the hotel entry. We discussed the coming adventure in Machu Picchu. Oscar had an illustrated guidebook, and explained the different temples and outlying buildings.

"This round slab was thought to be an astronomy post by the archaeologists, and the mount on top of it once had a large crystal for sky gazing. The big peak, Waynapicchu, is difficult to reach and has terracing high above. Do you see it in this photo?"

"Sure. Is it true they grew all their own food on those terraces?"

"Yes, the seeds were brought in by runners along the Royal Inca Road. This road connects above where the hotel is now, just outside the ruins. By the way, Caesar tells me there are no rooms available. What do you plan to do?"

"Well, Oscar, I heard from some guys from Toronto yesterday that there is a village called Aguas Calientes a couple of miles before the end of the line. They had just returned, and said that there are a couple of hostels with rooms there."

"That's right, but I want you to take care. The food and the hostels are really meager."

"I'll consider it an adventure," I replied.

"Okay, Jamie, but just remember to get back here in three days. Let's get back to this map."

As we pored over the pictures, Oscar told me the carvings in some walls were eroded but could still be seen in certain areas. He designated specific areas to go to for meditation so that I could get information from my own perceptions, rather than from what had been suspected by the guides and archaeologists.

Back in my room, I was bothered by his repeated warning about returning in three days. What did it mean? However, unwilling to waste energy thinking up something strange, I let it go.

I had to repack that evening so my bags could be stored in the hotel while I was gone. I was traveling light this time. I would have to carry my own luggage two miles to get to a place to stay for the night and, in this altitude, stamina and energy were hard to come by.

I did a quick meditation before bed, and my spirit lady began to speak to me again. She was such a comfort when she came. I wanted to thank her for her presence.

"Have you really watched me since I was a little girl?"

"Of course I have, and long before this life as well. I have learned from you, and you from me. It has been a beautiful exchange of energy. You see, little one, the important thing to remember is that within each being there is always a fight to decide between light and dark. Service to self and service to others. I have watched your fight, and have learned from your actions. We have chosen each other, and I find great joy in joining you in your quest for life. I am relearning the lessons of physical life through you. You will learn the lessons of spiritual life with my aid. In that way, we will quest together and I will always be with you."

PRIESTESS SONG

Sing sisters. . . sing!
    Raise your hearts high
    Greeting the gods
    That come from the sky.
Worship the rays
    That come from the sun
    Making our hearts
    beat together as one.
Honor the light
    That flows from moonbeams
    Pearl-like reflections
    That weave our dreams.
Bless the power
    Of the goddess within
    Walking in peace
    'Til eternity's end.
Sing sisters. . . sing!
    Raise your arms to the sun
    Reflecting the love
    Of The Ever-Living One.

— *Fifteen* —

The train to Machu Picchu was packed. I had heard about this train ride from a friend in Hollywood. It was one of the most famous rides in the world, because both ends of the train had an engine. The Andes were so radically high that it was necessary to traverse some of the peaks, and the train would run forward for a mile or so, then come to a stop. At that point, the power was switched and the train would go backwards, but move up to the next level of track at the same time. So much for people who get motion sickness! After a couple of hours of jaunting in this manner, we began a steady slow climb, paralleling the Inca Trail most of the way.

We saw groups of people hiking the Royal Road with guides, and others whitewater rafting the Urubamba River below. The Inca Trail was still in good shape and could be seen high above us to the left of the train. What was it that Oscar had told me?

"Jamie, the Incas were very evolved. It took only two-and-a-half hours for runners to go from one end of the empire to the other. They had relays, in which the swiftest of all the Indians carried messages or packages. If a scroll was not intact at the end of the line, they would be disgraced forever."

I thought about that when I looked high above me, and wondered why this excellent communication system had not worked against the Spaniards. Then I remembered that they had considered the Spaniards to be friends or gods. The Aztecs had made the same mistake.

Gazing out the window, I heard a giggle. It was one of the little girls from the hotel. Her long blonde hair and big green eyes startled me. "Where are the rest of the kids and your parents?" I asked.

"Oh, they're in the next car. We're going to stay at a hostel in Aguas Calientes for the night when we go to the ruins. Are you going to stay, too?"

"Yes, I am. Maybe we can all stay together."

"That would be fun. I'll go tell them." She giggled and ran down the aisle.

When we all piled off the train, buses waited to take us up the serpent-shaped road to the ruins nearly a mile above us. The Vilacanota River ran under the back of the station, and the buses had to cross the bridge over it before making the climb.

I was quickly introduced to the children's parents. There were two couples and another lady friend of theirs whose husband could not come. Carmen and Lalo were wonderful. We all checked our bags with the stationmaster before boarding the last bus. Lalo spoke English very well, and on the way up I learned that he was president of the University of the Pacifica in Lima. He had attended Stanford in California and was very interested in what I was trying to do here in Peru.

"Lalo, the doorway to space is somewhere up here and I intend to find it."

"Be sure to let us know if you find it. We are going to show the children all over the ruins. I respect your need to meditate, and we will meet with you later, okay?"

"That will be great. I feel like I need to look around the trail close to Waynapicchu. I'm very drawn to that area."

When we entered the ruins, I was flabbergasted. There were students and European tourists at every turn. One enters from the top and has to climb down steps that are eight to fifteen inches wide and six inches deep to reach the main open terrace. The city is shaped like a crater, in a sense, with terraces and buildings rising on three sides, and I found it very difficult to negotiate the tiny steps and passages filled with wall-to-wall people.

Trying a shortcut, I ended up in a small house-like structure — a dead end. Once again I had to climb three levels of worn stone steps and follow an endless line of tourists to get to the main trail. It led me to the open field in the center.

Finally I approached the open area and walked across the field. The grass was yellow and winter-dry, but in the center I saw roundish places, burned down to the earth beneath. Other areas were shaped the same way, but they had green grass growing about five inches high within their circumference. In total, there were about eight circles in this center area and on the other large terraced areas at the edge closest to the left of Waynapicchu. Crossing the lawn, I began to put the puzzle together. Some records indicated that this area was a meeting place for extraterrestrials, and that the Inca civilization had been colonized here.

So they are still landing here, I thought. I wonder why they come? Are they coming to see someone, or are they here to protect the ruins? Why would they protect ruins that are closed at night, unless there's something here that was left long ago? These thoughts racing through my mind, I walked to a ledge and sat down. I closed my eyes for a minute to see whether my spirit lady could help with the answers.

The psychic energy mounted inside me, and I was instantly dizzy. The world around me spun uncontrollably. I tried opening my eyes, with no luck. Fear darted in as I grabbed my stomach, trying to make the nausea subside. My eyes flew open and I was alone. No students, no tourists, just alone. I struggled to clear my vision. When I opened my eyes once more, about two hundred women, in flowing white dresses, were standing all around me on the terraces.

I was facing the canyon where the station sat, a mile below. With the river at the bottom and the ledge above, it seemed miles away. Where I sat was about three hundred yards from the cliff- like ledge. My psychic view was like a wide-angle camera lens. Hundreds of women stood with their backs to me. Every one of them had dark, flowing hair down to her hips. As the sun hit the backs of their heads, I saw highlights of chestnut, auburn, and blue- black.

They were singing a strange, chant-like song, their arms raised to the sky, watching something. I followed the angle. From the sky behind the peaks on the other side of the ravine came three small flying saucers, iridescent silver and fifteen to twenty feet across. They weren't flying, really, but simply floating. The grace of their movements left me spellbound as

I watched them descend to the open field in the center of the ancient city.

I stared in fascination, my ears allowing me to hear the soft chant of the harmonious female voices. I quickly glanced at the women. They, too, were facing the ships with their arms open, yet down towards the angle of the field. Shimmering rays of light emanated from the ships, flashing prisms of rainbow colors. Astonished, I suddenly realized that I was dressed in white, too. I felt the breeze lift me to my feet . . . this was too much! My heart was pounding, and I wanted to see what happened next, but I just felt limp.

I must have sat down again without looking, because the jolt brought me back into the present. I shook my head to clear it and found myself still in the same spot, with tourists milling around.

Someone sobbed softly, and I turned to my right. About twenty feet away was a fifty-year-old lady. Her red eyes and tear streaked face were puffed and lonely-looking. I walked over to her.

"Are you all right, Señora?"

"Oh, I'm so embarrassed. I don't know what is wrong with me. I can't stop crying. This place. . .this beauty. . .it's so familiar to me. I've never been here before. My grandchildren are over there somewhere. I don't want them to see me like this."

"I understand. Did you know that if you feel that way maybe you have been here before?"

"I was raised a Catholic and I still practice my faith, but I just know I have lived before."

"Senora, don't doubt what you feel. I know that I have been here before, too."

"You do? How do you know?"

I told her what I had seen just a few moments before, and she began crying again. I hugged and rocked her like a child until she could find stillness inside her.

"You are so kind. I'm sorry I got your sweater wet. What is your name? Mine is Rosa."

"I'm Jamie, Rosa. Are you doing okay now?"

"Oh yes, thank you so much. Come back later if you are

walking this way."

I kissed her on the cheek and said I would. I walked toward the back of the ruins, toward Waynapicchu. I needed to feel the earth under my feet and the sun on my face. All the places where Oscar had told me to go were mobbed. I needed to be alone. I could see those other places tomorrow.

The very difficult trail to the highest peak, Waynapicchu, took three to six hours to climb. The government required all hikers to sign in and out. I was already exhausted when I reached the thatched sign-in hut. "I'm sorry lady, no more today. The sun will set before the other hikers get back, so it is not allowed. Tomorrow, perhaps." I mumbled a thank-you and looked up the peak. Far-off specks of color caught my eye. Those specks were people.

Turning, I walked up the path to the far end of the field, just above the sign-out hut. I saw a stone house with a thatched roof, but was too tired to research what the guidebook called it. My head throbbing, I went in to escape the sun. One side of the hut was open like a stable, and inside was a lone white llama and her calf. Reaching in my bag, I fed her a piece of bread. A stray child walked up, wanting to pet her. The llama turned and hissed like a camel. I was surprised, until I remembered my zoology — llamas and camels are in the same family.

The hut was fast becoming a new gathering place for the tourists, so I took leave of the shade and walked to the cliff edge. I saw the train below, aware for the first time how high above the station I was. The eight-car train with two engines looked like a one-inch red caterpillar, only a sixteenth of an inch wide. That was the last look I needed! I turned back to the open field near this side of the jungle.

Feeling a presence behind me, I looked back. No one was there. I had gone to see the medium, Tom Massari, a few months before, to have a private session with Seth, the entity that Tom channels. Seth's words slowly came back to me. "A man will be there with you in spirit. A guide, in a sense. The doorway to space will be on your right. Do not step into it. If you feel it, move left."

My mind flashed back to the first moments after I had left Lalo. I had come to the entry point up the trail to the ancient city, but had taken a different road from the tourists. At the dead end, I had been alone. There I had raised my hand in the sign Oscar had shown me, and spoken the secret word three times.

Had that drawn this spirit guide to me? Sitting down on my parka, I tried to communicate with him.

"I can feel you behind me. Will you tell me who you are?"

The silence was pregnant with tingling emotion, but no words came. My heart was beating in my throat, and the cavity where my heart had been was filled with anticipation. I tried again.

"I really want to hear you. Do I know you?"

His voice was strong, yet soft, as his words penetrated my mind.

"I am Metegla. I was an Inca. A king. You were my child and had been chosen as one of the virgins to come to this city of temples. It was here that the daughters of man gave birth to the race of gods."

"What do you mean, the race of gods?"

"The Inca naton was ruled by a benevolent set of kings. The kings of our nation were born of human women who were made pregnant by the race from the sky. The ones who came to teach us peace. They left their mark in stone by Lake Titicaca. They are the ones who put life in the wombs of our virgin priestesses. You, my child, were one of these."

"Is that why Hiram Bingham and the others who discovered this city found skeletons of only women and children?"

"Yes. No men were allowed in the area except the runners sent from the capitol."

"This is a lot for me to handle and think on right now. I just want to get all the facts straight. Was the lady I met, Rosa, one of the priestesses too?"

"Yes, but in another time, later than your life here."

"I want to know about those saucers I saw in my vision. Where are they from? Were they fathers of the children born here?"

"I am not allowed to give you all the answers because you will

find some as you allow this journey of yours to unfold. I can tell you that during that time there were two groups of sky people. One was evil and used the symbols on the Nazca plains to terrorize the people of our nation, making their presence felt through fear. The other group was sent to seed our people with love. The children born from these unions were taught equality and tenderness for others. These beings gave life to the bellies of our women by having the women stand in the light that shone from their bodies. It was from such a union that I was born. There was no physical union, for the bodies of the sky people were not made of flesh."

"What about the evil group, were they flesh?"

"The group of which you speak was from the place your people call Orion. Their ships were not those you saw. They were dark-pewter colored and their bodies were solid. That is why they were able to lead the Spaniards to the capitol and bring our nation to her knees."

My head reeling, I was unable to withstand the intensity of the information any longer. I told Metegla that I was going to walk to the cafeteria at the hotel above.

There was only silence. . . he was gone.

I was late for lunch. The line was still open, but the selection was poor. Sitting with my canned fruit cup and Inca Cola, looking at the watery chicken stew, I wanted to cry.

"Nobody would ever believe what I just heard, nobody! This is outrageous, but I know in my heart it's true. I just can't tell anyone. I'll have to be very silent and just know for myself," I thought.

To my left was a table of "seven days and six nights" tourists from the States, the only American group I had seen there. I looked at their polyester pantsuits and started to laugh inside. If those people could only hear what I just had, I bet they would take the first flight home and check into Rosalyn Carter's program for better mental health!

A bit of canned grapefruit stuck in my throat and I nearly choked. I was coughing and leaning over the pink fiberglass picnic bench when Lalo appeared. As I recovered, I decided to dive in and see what his reaction would be if I told him just a tiny bit of what I had seen in the vision.

I related what I had seen — the women and the saucers — and he seemed mildly interested, so I continued.

"I think the reason that they found only women and children here was because it was a place for the high priestesses to mate with extraterrestrials."

There it was, out of my mouth. I watched his face. He seemed puzzled. I wondered if he was puzzled about my sanity! He said another curious thing.

"Well, anything is possible. Here in my country we have had many strange things happen. You are familiar with the Nazca plains, no doubt?" I nodded. "There have been many of the mountain people who have had encounters with those beings from the outer space. Some places here in the Andes, they are known for the beings that come at night."

His English was so cute when he was thinking faster than he could put the words together.

"Jamie, did you hear about our Lake Titicaca on the Bolivian border?"

"I have just recently heard of it, Lalo." I smiled to myself. So the unfoldment and my answers were coming very quickly!

"Recent findings have proven that the giant stone there is a calendar. It was very strange, and they took a long time to figure it out. The scientists know now that it is the solar calendar of Venus."

"Venus! Oh, that is really wild," I thought.

I started telling him about the pictures on my forehead that had appeared from time to time, including the most recent ones which seemed to apply to Peru. Right before I had flown to Lima, on the last day at Terí's house, the pictures had come again. I was not familiar with what they meant. The friends who had come for coffee at Terí's had seen them too, as if they had been painted on my skin. They were becoming visible to others.

Lalo and I headed for the hostel to check in, and the whole group of parents and kids set out for the buses. Collecting our bags below, we started the trek to Aguas Calientes. The kids sang and counted the railroad ties as we walked. It was nearly sunset, and the shadows were long beside the river.

I had bought two small strings of Peruvian turquoise from a little girl named Ruth. She had been brown as a berry and quite small for a fourteen-year-old. I giggled when I thought about how sweetly she offered her wares, but how suddenly she changed and would swear if the tourists turned her down. She would turn on a dime and begin cursing like a sailor until she found a new buyer, her black eyes shining or becoming blacker if she got a "no thank you." I was attracted to her spunk, and was very happy with my turquoise as I felt the smoothness of the stones in my hand. I smiled, slipped them into my jacket, and listened to them jingle. The harmony was lovely, with the children's voices echoing off the canyon walls and the river bubbling to my right.

The villagers seemed curious as our entourage entered town. Some smiled and waved, and we waved back. The hostel was bearable, but not terrific. The rooms had bunks for students and were clean, but the baths in the hall were cold, smelled of urine, and had no toilet paper. I cashed in on buying some at the desk in the lobby.

After pasta and soup, we all sat and talked. The children were fascinated with the idea of pictures on my forehead. We went to the lobby, parents in tow, and started to play a game of telepathy. I used the circle, square, triangle, and star as symbols. We wrote one down and all the kids would focus on which one it was. They were amazingly accurate.

I decided to get out the journal with my notes and drawings. Lalo was the first to speak up when we reached the pictures I had drawn in Mexico City.

"Do you see this one here?" he pointed. "It is the sun symbol above the Portal del Sol at Lake Titicaca. And this one here is from the Nazca plains. . . the other one there is the head of a bull, designed to ward off evil spirits; that is carved in stone at Titicaca."

"That's remarkable to me, Lalo. I would have never known if you hadn't told me, because on this trip I will only be returning to Cusco, and then back to Mexico."

"How many more days do you intend to be here, Jamie? You realize that we are going home tomorrow, yes?"

"I'll be here another two days. I wish you were all staying as well."

"I must return to the University. Carmen would love to stay longer, but business is business, you know."

We talked and played games for an hour or two longer before they all kissed me goodnight. We were to meet early for breakfast and then walk to the ruins. We all wanted to arrive early, before the mob. Each day, most of the tourists left the mountain at three thirty by the return tourist train. The hotel on top had accommodations for only forty doubles.

That night I was freezing and cursed the lack of heat. I kept waking, stiff from the cold, and finally stole the blanket from the unoccupied bunk above me.

The minute the sun hit the window I was up and to the bathroom. Forget bathing fully, not a drop of hot water! I quickly dressed and headed for breakfast, but the hot chocolate and stale roll with marmalade didn't exactly perk me up. Soon, however, we were all together, fed, and on our way.

We were the only people on the tracks at first, but then some of the mountain women arrived, carrying their enormous loads. I had read that with no pack animals, unspoken rules in this culture dictated that the women were the work horses. I believed it now.

The stationmaster hadn't arrived, and we had quite a wait. No one was happy about that, since the train wouldn't pull into the station for an hour or so. All the people wanting to get to the ruins before the masses arrived were grumbling.

Finally the train arrived and we reached our destination. At the top of the ruins, we all went our separate ways, planning to meet for lunch. I went to the entrance and once again said the secret word three times, holding my hand in the manner Oscar had shown me. I then entered, and visited all the places Oscar had recommended, finding several of my own besides.

All the buildings in the ruins were structurally small, and I realized that although the present race here in the mountains was very short, they must have grown some since these ancient times.

I headed for the side where I had been the previous day. On the second terrace, above the open field, I spread my parka and began to meditate. Suddenly Metagla's voice boomed in my ears, just as it had the day before.

"So you are doubting yourself and that I am really here with you?"

He was right. I had thought about it every time I woke up during the night. "Oh, dear, I guess I'm going to get chewed out," I thought.

"No child, you are not," came the answer. *"Your doubts are natural. This is the time in your development to doubt. Look to your right at that bamboo. There is an entrance to subterranean walkways there. Go look."* Metagla's voice faded away.

I walked to the bamboo twenty yards to my right, and there truly was a hole. The air coming up from it was very wet and cold. I moved to the right side for a better view, and saw what looked like old, broken steps. Oh, boy, another secret that could help the archaeologists find some new evidence about the history here, I thought.

I turned to get my coat, and saw Lalo and Carmen a hundred yards away. I yelled and they came over with three of the children in the group.

As we were all looking at my new discovery, the guard arrived, very upset. He warned us not to get too close. Maybe it would cave in, he said, or someone would fall in and we wouldn't be able to reach her. He called for the archaeologist on duty while we talked about what the hole could be.

Lalo told me that many underground passages had been found in Inca lands, and that it was possible that this was yet another one. The archaeologist was off-duty, so we had to move away from the hole. The guard stood there, unmoving, so that we would have to leave.

I waved "so long" to Carmen and Lalo as I cut across the open field to the place where the crystal had been. The archaic observatory. These women must have been seers. They had to know when the ships would come. When I got to the top of the terraces on the other side, there were so many peo-

ple there that I decided to leave. The clouds were coming in
and the sun was behind them. My body was stiff from all the
climbing and from never getting warm enough, but I had a
bus to catch and two miles to walk.

Down at the tracks I again saw Ruth, the little girl who had
sold me the turquoise. I headed to the hostel, and she ran up,
asking if I wanted to buy any more jewelry. I got a little pair of
earrings made from some old half-soles, equal to a half-
penny, and began my trek. What a day this had been! I wanted
to be able to breathe better, but the air was so thin that I just
decided to walk slowly.

This was the day on which all the villagers were waiting
for me. I had been dreading the bleak hostel, with nobody to
talk to, and all these people were waiting for me. I had never
seen them before. They kept whispering that the madonna
was coming.

The little boy with the club foot who had been pushed out
in front of me was named George. I worked with him for half
an hour, telling him to feel the power of the Creator and lay-
ing my hands on his legs and feet. I told him, the best way I
knew how, that the foot would take time to heal. He nodded.

It seemed like hours passed as, one after another, the
villagers came in throngs. I was working in an open plaza in
front of the alcalde's — the Mayor's — house. They had no
medical treatment here. Some people just wanted me to talk
to them and reassure them that they weren't going to die
young. Others asked about loved ones, and still others came
for healing.

By this time the trains for the day had long since passed,
and mist trailed into the canyon in a slow-moving, wispy white
cloud. Ruth was at my side, hoping to get her fortune told, and
proud of having the Americana as her friend.

Ruth suggested that because of the cold we go to a tiny,
three-table cafe about a hundred feet across the track. I
agreed, since it was now pitch-black outside, and the people
all followed. Exhausted, I ate what they called a small pizza, a
six-inch round piece of bread dough, rolled flat and smeared
with tomato paste, and with a handful of goat or llama cheese

on top. It hit the spot, and the coca tea, called *mate* (ma·teh), warmed my insides. Later that night I stumbled up to the hostel, ready to drop.

The climb to my room felt like it would be my last one in this world. Flower beds set into the side of the hill bloomed with tropical fuchsia flowers. I wondered if I were dreaming. In this cold, could it be? The last turn to the building finally came, and then two more flights of steps. I don't even remember undressing or going to bed.

Morning was a real drag. I was molded into a fetal position. My muscles ached so badly that I even hurt between my toes. My hair needed a wash, but that was out of the question. I had one fleeting thought about climbing the hill to the mineral bath, but that too faded when my body moved to the edge of the bunk and my feet hit the cold cement floor.

Even my thick socks seemed frozen. With supreme effort I dressed and brushed my teeth, the stench of urine burning in my nostrils. I nearly gagged, and thought, "better not." I had to go to the bathroom, and trekked across the hall again to get my toilet paper. "Nothing like being prepared, Miss Sams," I whispered angrily to myself. Most of the toilet doors were broken, and as these were co-ed bathrooms, I decided to try holding the door closed with my foot.

While I was in the john, a married couple came in, half-naked, to take a cold shower as I made my first sound. They were embarrassed, covering themselves as I dashed past them. My face was beet-red. So much for liberation in the twentieth century!

Deciding to eat at the ruins, I hurriedly made my way to the station. I was alone on the tracks, since it was midday. Ten in the morning is midday in the Andes, because all tourists are at the ruins and all the natives are at the bottom of the station, waiting to sell to the tourists. It is their only hope of cash.

After a quick breakfast, I decided to return to the trail leading to Waynapicchu. Signing in, I headed down into a small valley that was really just a dip before the serious climb to the top. About three hundred yards down the trail, I stumbled and fell hard. The shooting pain was intense and I couldn't move for a minute. I thought I had broken something, but the parts all moved. That did it!

I was crazy with pain, cursing myself for being so clumsy. I tried to move and slowly got up. My ankle was turned, but not really sprained. My upper thigh was another thing altogether — I must have pulled a tendon or ripped a muscle. I thought I was never going to make it back to the hut to sign out. Every step on this trail was two feet high and was, in truth, a hurdle for me. It took me an hour to return the short distance.

I hobbled up to the terrace after signing in again and sat about ten feet from where I had discovered the hole, crying like a baby. Now I would never see the Temple of the Moon! Everyone had to leave by three-thirty. I was going back to Cusco the next day and hadn't even bought my ticket. "This is ridiculous and I just don't care," I thought, tears streaming down my face. I was too embarrassed to try to move.

For the next hour, I tried to sort out my feelings and get myself calm enough to meditate. The terraces were still filled with tourists. Big grey clouds rolled in and I saw that it was going to rain. "Oh, God, how am I going to get out of here!" Nothing was right; everything was wrong. I tried to get up and stand. Looking around at the beautiful, quaint buildings, I bid them goodbye. It took me another hour to cross the field and negotiate the high steps on the other side. It had started sprinkling.

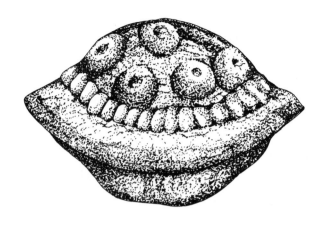

GOODBYE

I knew always
    that you would go. . .
       and far away. . .
But I didn't know that the sun
    was really a bright black. . .
And the moon,
       only a reflection of your eyes.

— *Sixteen* —

I was on firm ground. My body was shaking. The train...the train. Those tunnels. Ruth...where is Ruth!

"Ruth!"

Was I screaming, thinking, or praying? We weren't dead, were we?

"Yes, Señorita? You see it's okay. We are here, safe and sound. Señorita, you are pale. Come, let's get you some coca tea. The train is gone. She went back to Cusco. Come."

All I could remember seeing was the reflection of Ruth's face as we had approached the first tunnel, afraid that she would be killed because she was outside the train. I was in a time warp. The prayers had worked. The engine still pounded in my ears. The crush of the metal door had left an imprint on my chest, and I was totally numb. I was faint and shaking at the same time. Dazed, I wondered what promises I had made to the Maker that were in need of keeping now.

The next thing I knew, I was sitting in the tin-roofed cafe across the tracks, the owner bellowing that I was soaked and hurrying me in front of the tiny brick chimney. I glanced around to see the firelit orifice which also served as the pizza oven, but I couldn't get warm with the amount of fire it held. It took nearly an hour to cook a quarter-inch crust. I was soaked to the bone, and things weren't getting any better. I was still in shock and couldn't even entertain the thought of moving.

The rough-hewn tables and benches scattered around the room were empty. In the far corner, on two stools, sat a European couple in their early thirties. They were deep in impassioned conversation, and I couldn't help wondering if they were real. Everything seemed so alien to me, and the setting and the kerosene light made it nightmarish. It was all I could do to slug down a cup or two of coca tea.

I looked up to see several faces at the ancient wooden

door, which had been salvaged from some bygone building. The next few hours seemed surrealistic as, robot-like, I did readings or healings for one after another of the Indios. My chest grew tight, and the tickle in my throat wasn't helping me feel very confident. I knew for sure that I was going to be sick, but something kept driving me to finish. Long after midnight the last of the villagers left, and Ruth led me to the hostel in a daze.

I had to get back to Cusco. I kept trying to remember how I had been able to get a ticket. Then it came to me. I had broken the fever of the stationmaster's grandbaby. In gratitude, he had arranged for me to travel on a special two-car business train to Cusco. He wore "coke-bottle" glasses and lived above the station. He and his wife had asked me to come a little early and do a quick reading for them before the train left the next day. I could only hope that I would be able to remember in the morning.

In my room, I peeled off the wet clothes and piled on layers of dry long-johns, with my flannel nightgown on top. I pulled all the bedding from the bunk above, piling it on top of me. My chest ached and it was becoming hard to breathe. Frightened, and very tired, I pulled the covers over my head to breathe air that was a little warmer.

A sudden thought struck me: I had forgotten the password and secret sign today. Was that why it had all been so awful? As I closed my eyes, the tears I had been trying to hold in check spilled over my lashes.

I had cursed my body many times in the past. The physical strength that I needed was just not there. I felt the same way I had in Palm Springs — inadequate. There was an intense pain in my lungs and I was sure that if I did not get some kind of help I would leave my body forever. My breath was shallow and I was shaking with chills and fever. The nearest medical facility was a first aid station on top in Machu Picchu. That was out of the question. They didn't even have a doctor as far as I knew. Cusco was five hours by train, and the train did not come until tomorrow.

During the night I would sleep for a few minutes, and

then wake up in pain without being able to breathe. This continued until I resorted to the only thing I knew to do — pray. Pray that I wouldn't die here alone in this mud hostel away from everyone I loved.

I cried out into the universe and asked the Great Spirit to aid me. "If anyone can hear me, please help me. I don't want to die and I know that I am here to help people and heal my planet. . . please!" I screamed. Everyone was gone. This floor of the hostel was empty. All of the tourists were back in their homes; the weekend was over. If I had ever believed in the power of God, I needed to believe in it now. I briefly opened my eyes and blinked back the tears of frustration and anger and fear. I tried to calm myself and wait.

Closing my eyes again, I saw seven tiny, round-headed beings putting their hands inside my body up to their elbows. I felt something being moved near my lungs and chest.

Their bodies were white and transparent, and their eyes large and kind, with heavy upper and lower lids. Their noses were obscure, with only the nostrils showing above tiny, thin-lipped, slit-like mouths.

The tallest of them was about four feet high; others were three to three-and-a-half feet high. Certain that I was dreaming, I opened my eyes with a start. They were still there! I was so shaken by their presence that I tried to move. One of them said, "Relax, please. We will help you. We are from Reticulum. You are very ill. Be still." I could feel the organs in my body being moved, and a serenity coming over me.

The little man to my right telepathically said to another one across my body to the left, "It's her lungs, one has collapsed. We will have to take her to the ship."

At that moment it all began to feel like a dream. I was nearly blinded by a bright light, and felt my body being lifted through the solidity of the upper bunk and the ceiling. I could see the silver disc of the ship above me and a large opening. When I closed my eyes all I could see was a very bright electric blue ray of light piercing my third eye and entering my brain. It seemed like a communication ray and was very comforting.

Inside the ship I was placed on a table and was touched gently. My heart was feeling pressured in its effort to get enough oxygen. The tiny man that had spoken to me before once again put his voice in my head.

"We are moving you to the station inside the big mountain to get the proper help. Be calm and all will be well."

Tears rolled down my eyes and I sent him my thanks telepathically. After that there was a blank spot in my memory, because the next thing I knew was that I was under very bright lights and was looking into the faces of five more beings from Zeta Reticuli. A long object was hanging over me, similar to the arm of a dentist's drill and with tubes connected to it. The pain in my chest was much easier and I was feeling the relief.

The little man invaded my thoughts again and told me that they had fixed my lung but that my body was very infected and it would have to fight this off on its own. I was not going to die. In some way I felt very clear, and was aided in sitting up.

I wanted to see what was around me and get oriented to my surroundings. I was on a balcony of some sort that was glassed in a few feet high with a rail around it. I started to stand and realized that I was only about 24 inches off the floor. As I stood up I saw the inside of a huge cavern with very bright lights. About twenty spacecraft were on a white polished floor. There were other beings walking around on the landing pad as well. They were like earthlings, but very tall.

In the far left corner was a beautiful blonde woman in a silver dress that had a shiny metallic blue cape over it. Her hair was wavy and cascaded down to her shoulders. She wore a helmet that was silver and came to a point like a widow's peak in the front. The sides of the helmet had golden wings inlaid upon the surface. I was staring at her in fascination when she suddenly stopped and turned straight towards me. I couldn't believe my eyes. She smiled and winked at me.

She crossed the two or so acres of space to meet me as I, in turn, walked down a set of stairs to meet her. No telepathy was needed — she talked to me.

"Would you like a tour?"

"Why yes, if it isn't too much trouble," I replied.

I remember her taking me all over the landing space and then leading me to some caves that were connected by tunnels. Inside these caves were beautiful pieces of Inca statuary made of gold. Many of the caverns were filled with masks, artifacts, solar discs, and much more. I asked her why it was all here.

"The temple priestesses of long ago hid it here for the future. It will be used in the right way again," she answered.

"What is the right way?" I asked.

"The original intent was to use these objects for healing. They will be needed again in the age to come when there is no need for money or possessions. Your people will one day come to the understanding that life is the most precious gift you have, and that life comes only from one Source. The Incas were taught by us that all life comes from the Source, and in this solar system that Source is the sun.

"It is the light that is reflected from God that sets your sun alight and gives you the sustenance you need. That same sunlight was reflected in the gold used to adorn these ancient cities. As in Egypt, Mexico, and with the cities of Cibola, it was also used to heal those in need. The frequency of gold was also used by your alchemists to heal spiritual ills. In your life you will see it used again."

She walked me to the door of a ship where the others were waiting, and told me that I must return and rest.

In a half-sleeping state I heard myself say that this must have been a really wild dream, but I was aware that the pain was gone, and that my lungs didn't hurt anymore.

My travel alarm had just rung. I was not moving, and a huge weight sat on my chest. I tried to sit up, but a wave of dizziness hit me. I was burning with fever. My leg still ached, and I had to catch that morning train. I had to get medical attention. Sheer will and one-minded persistence got me up and to the station. I was coughing up infection, sitting outside in the cold, when the stationmaster finally came to the weatherworn door.

He led me through the station to a downstairs room

where one of his children slept. The walls were crumbling and the newspaper-plugged holes didn't block the cold. The ceiling was fourteen feet above and had one naked light bulb hanging in its center, lighting the baby-blue paint covering most of the adobe walls. The child slept on as the station-master fetched hot tea, using the only cup on the tiny yellow table next to the bed. The painted wooden table was chipped and about to fall apart, so I tried not to bump it as I sat.

My voice was a hoarse whisper as I told him I would wait for the coca tea and for his wife to get up. When he returned with the battered enamel cup full of tea, dead ants floated on the top. I was so embarrassed that I didn't want to mention it. The man was legally blind, and it had taken forever to get the water hot in the first place. I tried to be calm and wait for his wife. When he wasn't looking, I skimmed off some of the ants and drank deeply. After all, they ate them in Europe covered with chocolate, I told myself.

The Señora arrived and I did three quick readings for the stationmaster, his wife, and daughter. I prayed that the train would come soon. Just as I finished the last reading, the daughter called to us that the train had pulled in.

I was deposited on the first car, next to an Argentinean student on holiday. He and his friend saw that I was sick, and when we got to Cusco, they made sure I made it to the hotel.

I was trying to sign in when the manager came and said that there were no more rooms. That was the last straw. I started crying. Caesar Tejeira found me crying and arranged for my room. The doctor was called.

I ordered hot chocolate, and while waiting for the doctor I took a hot bath, bundled up, and climbed into bed. Shaking with fever, I spent some very long hours before he arrived. I had turned up the heat full blast. A few of the employees for whom I had done readings stopped by, looking worried. They ordered more blankets and hot tea. They had been waiting for my return — but not like this. I was dying, or so I thought.

The doctor arrived and turned down the heat. The room was sweltering. My temperature read 104 degrees on my American thermometer. He sent a bellboy to the pharmacy and gave me a shot of antibiotics. "Here is your other medicine," he said, handing me four more boxes.

"What are these?"

"Those are four more shots of penicillin. Here are your needles. If you need to, you can call me in a few days."

"Wait a minute! What am I supposed to do with these shots? Give them to myself?"

"Yes, that would be fine, or you can call the desk. One of the clerks knows how to give them."

"Are you serious? You mean you're leaving me to myself or a clerk?"

"Why yes, Miss Sams. What else would you have me do?"

"Okay mister. . .that's fine. Here's your money. Thirty dollars, right?"

"That is correct. I will check on you, if you wish."

"For thirty dollars, I wish!"

One of the girls at the hotel had already told me that the standard price was twelve dollars. This doctor's fee was highway robbery! I was confused about whether I felt angry or helpless. This situation was new for me. I would have to be my own nurse.

After three days of sleep, high fever, and times of not knowing whether I was awake or asleep, the maitre'd and his wife took me to their doctor. I had pneumonia. I had been giving myself the shots, mixing the liquid with the powdered antibiotic before drawing it into the syringe. My rear end was a mass of bruises where I had missed a few times, but I was alive.

I couldn't leave because, except for the flight I had previously booked in Los Angeles, there were no unreserved seats for two months. This was too much of a nightmare to be believed! I would have to wait until my scheduled departure one week away.

After the fourth day and the second doctor's pills, my fever was down to 100. Oscar called, wanting to take me to the secret temples at the ruins outside of town. I was eating a little and feeling better, so I agreed. That was not a bright decision.

We had to go several miles by taxi and have the not-so-happy driver return for us an hour or two later. We had walked a mile and I had just crumbled. I had no breath and was crying. It had started to rain, so Oscar settled me inside the hidden fertility temple while he went to find the cabby. These temples are set into the ruins, where the tourists never see them. Located outside Cusco, these Inca buildings stood where the Spaniards raped tons of gold from the rocks, stealing it from the people.

I took a picture inside and at the entrance, where an elephant head was visible but had been defaced by the Spaniards. The grey stone was carved in a perfect elephant shape, the trunk forming a handrail to the entrance. The hidden opening behind it was in the shape of a human vaginal cavity. I felt very strange walking into the temple. The impression I got was one of entering the creative channel of the earth mother. It was more like a cave, and reminded me of Carlsbad Caverns in New Mexico on a very small scale. In front of me was a brightly-lit round slab of smooth stone, illuminated by a hole in the top of the cavern. It was eerie to experience the amount of light this created, even when it was cloudy outside. The cave was so dark that any light coming in was reflected by the round, white stone table.

I felt a presence in the temple with me, then disregarded it. Oscar had returned without finding the cabby, and said that it would be a while. He explained that the stone slab was where the babies had been birthed. The light from above gave the midwives enough light to work, but protected the children from the strong rays of the sun until they adjusted to their new world. I decided to take a photo of this marvelous birthing chamber. It was almost exactly like the stone bed I had see inside the hollow mountain in Palm Springs.

After we had seen the major parts of the various inner workings of the ruins, Oscar asked if I could walk a bit to find the taxi. I agreed to do it just to calm myself, since I was feeling sick again.

We walked a few hundred feet, but the pain in my lungs returned. The sharpness of some of the pulsations hammered blood into my ears, and I gasped for air that just could not enter my pulmonary system. I was about to ask Oscar to stop when the intermittent rain started up again. We had reached an open field which had three-foot-high stone borders on each side of the mud road on which we were walking. He stopped.

"Jamie, what do you feel psychically in this spot?"

I was stunned. I could barely speak for lack of oxygen, my body vibrated with pain, and Oscar wanted me to try to tune into a spot in the road! I began sobbing. As I cried, the impression I received was of gallons of blood covering the entire field. The neutral color of the rocks and earth beneath me became bright red.

"Oscar, all I see is blood. This was a battlefield where the Incas were murdered by the Spaniards!" I wheezed.

"Can't you see beyond that? There was beauty here before that time. Why are you picking up the worst part of the history?"

I yelled, "All I want to do is go home! I can't breathe and I feel awful! Can't you see that? Please take me home!"

The tears were streaming down my face and I was gasping for breath. Oscar's face became stoical and his manner abrupt. He told me to wait while he found the taxi. The ride back was silent.

At the hotel, I was informed that they would have to find me another hotel because they needed my room, now that I was better. They moved me to a tiny hostel on the main plaza the next day, and I was in bed there for another two days. The mountain air was very bad for lung problems, and I was not getting any better.

From my hostel window, I watched throngs of people outside bargaining with street vendors. I looked at the cathedral across the plaza. I slept and dreamed. Everything was tan. The plaza, the houses, the land, the grass, the faces: all were the same. I began to understand why they all wore such bright colors.

The Hostel Wiracocha was not terrific. It was only a two-star hostel, but I was happy just to have hot water and a phone. As the days rolled by before my departure, I went out only briefly with my new friends from the big hotel to eat or see the doctor. I was content to take it easy and reflect on what I had learned. Oscar came to my room one day with one of his developing psychics.

"Jamie, you have a bad character trait when you are ill."

"I know that I'm impatient, Oscar, but I felt as if I were going to die out there on the plain near the ruins! I couldn't breathe and I had no strength to walk the necessary miles to the second set of ruins. I hope you understand. I'm really sorry."

"It's okay. You have never told me what happened up there in Machu Picchu. Did you use the sign and password?"

"Yes, all except the last day. That's when I got hurt and ill."

"You are being awfully silent. I know that something happened, but you aren't saying."

"Oscar, I'm so tired and sick that I can't even think well enough in Spanish to be able to tell you."

The dark young man whom Oscar had brought stared at me, and gave me his psychic impressions.

"You were involved in some type of fertility ceremony in a life in Machu Picchu. Your color was red, and I see you with a many-feathered headdress. You were in some type of Gnostic rites having to do with love-making."

"What are you talking about? I don't understand. Are you saying that I was a priestess of a sex temple?"

"Not exactly, Señorita. But I keep on seeing that you made babies for the Inca King."

Well, that cinched it. I was very uncomfortable. This student saw part of what I had seen at the big mountain. I was lost in thought, and not one Spanish phrase would come to mind to try to explain to either of them what I had experienced.

The words forming in my mind were a babel of French, English, Spanish, and Italian. No way could I think, much less speak. I just sat on the tiny bed and stared past the two men into a mirror in the bathroom that reflected the blankness of the beige ceiling.

They talked of other things until I was so befuddled that I had to sleep. I felt I was losing touch with this wonderful friend who had tried so hard to show me the secrets of the Incas. All I could think of was flying back to Mexico and seeing Teri and Raul. I was so constipated from the antibiotics that I was nauseated every time I saw food.

Two days before leaving Cusco, I went to dinner at the best cabaret and restaurant in town with Caesar Tejeira and his wife. Relieved to have my appetite back, I ordered the trout with garlic sauce. I was up all night with food poisoning. I left Peru thinking that if I had stayed a day longer, I would have been killed in some way or another!

Mexico was just the ticket to render me fairly rested until I could get home. I slept and was taken care of at Teri's house. I relaxed with the family, enjoying a lot of quiet time with them. I was still not well, and I began to ponder. A few weeks in bed, my own bed, would give me plenty of time to think and review what had happened to me. So many pieces were missing.

COSMIC CARD GAME

Wholeness comes
   When you begin to believe
      You create the lessons
         and learn to receive.
The cards *you* dealt
   to allow you to grow.
Then you stop thinking. . .
      You just feel. . .and KNOW.

— Seventeen —

I had a month of mail to answer, and a month of phone calls to return. I also had to heal the haunting memories of what had happened to me at the end of my trip.

Was I trying to unconsciously hurt myself because I felt I had failed? I had certainly done a bang-up job of it! I had been so off-center that I had either forgotten to meditate or felt too sick to do it. That, of course, is usually when one needs it the most.

I was almost well by now, and it was time. I no sooner began to meditate than the Voice came to me.

"How are you, little one?"

"I'm fine now. I just have a little confusion regarding the trip."

"There are parts that you do not totally remember due to the fact that you were so ill, child."

"Can you help me tie it together? I was wondering why Oscar warned me not to stay more than three days in Machu Picchu?"

"Señor Tejeira is very psychic. He psychically saw you dying if you had stayed, due to lack of medical attention. That is why he gave you the passwords and signs."

"You mean he saw me dying of pneumonia before I went?"

"It was more than that. If you had climbed to the Temple of the Moon high above the city, he feared you would fall to the bottom of Waynapicchu."

"But why would I have fallen?"

"In your lifetime there, it was the supreme test of initiation to go to the Temple of the Moon at night. At the top there is a tunnel you must pass through, and at the end there is a sharp turn. On the night of the new moon, the initiates were sent through the tunnel one at a time. If one allowed fear to take hold and was not in the

present, the turn would not be obvious in the darkness. If one walked straight ahead, one would fall a mile to the bottom of the canyon. You had allowed that fear to rule you when you lost your life during initiation. What happened at the bottom of the trail saved you from being in that situation again. You are not ready yet. Your strength needs to be tested by you. You knew this on some level of conscious-ness and created the alternate lesson below."

Chills ran through me, and I flashed on the fear of falling I had always had. I had fallen from a two-story building in San Luis Potosí, Mexico in 1973 and had broken my back. So I had repeated, in a sense, the lessons of other lives. I wanted to know more.

"Why did I not get in touch with the archaeologist at Machu Picchu? I had to relate what I had found to a guy I met in the cafe the day before I left. His name was David Drew — an archaeologist from England."

"Your ego was in the way. You believed it would help you get into the psychic community more securely. You were not thinking of the data that could help others, just of yourself, until you had gone through the illness. You made the right decision after you had created a situation that made you see what was really important to you. That was life and sharing. Your pathway was to understand that you are an instrument. The discovery is to be another's. You did your part."

She was right on every count so far. The lessons had been high drama, and so dangerous that I had to look at my value system. My curiosity expanded.

"Where do you fit into all of these scenarios?"

"I have been your spiritual teacher for many lifetimes. I am Leah. I am from the planet of Venus. I come to you in love. I am a humble servant of the light. You will be able, now that you have cleared your own channel through soul-searching, to use my energy and teachings to aid others — if you choose."

I was nearly paralyzed. If I choose? How could I *not* want to help others and myself! How could I not want to channel her energy! She was the one who had led me on the journey, and helped me find and heal myself. Now the connection be-tween the ancients and the sky brothers was clear to me.

"Oh Leah, yes — yes. I do want to be a channel. I do want to help others. I have so much to learn. Will I be a good channel?"

"To the degree that you open your heart in love. To the degree that you allow the Creator's love to be reflected within you. To the degree that your ego allows you to serve others as a part of the whole."

"I will work hard. I want so much to be of service. I want my life to count for something. I want to discover the secrets of the universal Force. I want to help bring peace to the Family of Man."

"Listen, child, you must rid yourself of the past and learn to be in the moment. You must love yourself and be gentle as you learn. Do not set goals that are impossible to accomplish alone. Seek unity. Awareness is perception, and the allowance of all things to unfold in their own time and space."

"I understand. I will try." My words seemed to have an understated vacant ring.

"It is in growing and unfolding that you will experience all sides of your whole. Focus on the last moments with Ruth when you started getting ill. Do you remember?"

"I think I do. I was in a state of shock."

"Yes, and you were not in the moment. You kept on pushing with a fury to see all those who had come to see you. Service to others means taking care of yourself so that you can continue to serve. You do not remember the words from the innkeeper, do you?"

"No, but let me try to recall — it will just take a minute."

The scene came flashing back as I focused my attention on that tiny cafe. It had been very late, and only five people were left. They had asked if I were going to come back again. I had told them that I would, someday. Ruth had looked at me in a very curious way, and then had said, "Señorita, we will miss your visits. They help us so much."

"Ruth what do you mean, my visits?"

"You know what I mean. You have been here once every three months for the past year."

I had believed when she said this that I was losing my sense of coherence. Now it struck me like a jolt of electricity. I asked Leah to explain.

"You have been operating your double since then. They all knew you. That is why they called you the madonna. 'The Lady' was your only name before this trip."

"You are saying that I have been in two places at one time?"

"Yes, it is an ability that comes when one can separate levels of consciousness and create on a level known as the causal plane. You have done well."

"Leah, I have had so much happen to me that I feel I cannot tell anyone about. My friend Molly was right years ago. This is my private storm."

"You only fear that others will think you to be mad. That, my child, is ego. Your personality will never be wounded by the truth. You cannot be harmed by what others choose to believe unless you are carrying an idea of 'who you are' that is measured by the ideas of others."

She was right. Busted again! I guess I needed that. Leah continued.

"There will be many who will try to attack what you are saying, due to the fact that they are not comfortable with who they are or their own beliefs. It is not for anyone to judge the actions of others. Each being is doing the best it can to create life lessons for itself. My people carry the love that allows all beings to see peace. Peace within themselves and the universe. We have come to be of assistance so that all beings in this universe may find that those answers are within themselves."

"But Leah, I feel such urgency. I feel like I will never have enough time to do all that is needed."

"Time is created as an illusion to allow all beings to mark the changes in their realities. You will have the time you need. Zealotism has caused many in your world to go to war. This is the beginning of a new age of understanding. Those that would seek answers will be attached to truth that applies to their present state of awareness. In every situation, there is as much learning as there is teaching. The secret is in finding joy in your own growth and respecting the ideas and growth of others."

"I feel like there is much for me to learn. I want to grow

and I want to help, but I feel so inadequate."

"Oh, little one, you must first learn that all things are equal. Each idea in the universe has its own validity and purpose. So it is with human beings. Each person is a thread in a grand tapestry. Each carries a unique sound, color, and light. Without one single idea or living organism, the tapestry would not be whole. The teacher in you is emerging and the road will be long. Enjoy the weavings of your path. Your work is equal to all others. Do not judge it or yourself. Love the dips in the pathway, as well as the rises, and you will find the wholeness you seek."

"I will remember your words. I must begin to try to live this way. The learning will be my task. Will you teach and help me?"

"I am with you every time you need my presence. If you look closely at the photograph you took inside the fertility temple when you were alone, you will see my face."

I quickly rifled through my desk for my box of pictures, just back from the developers. Half of them were on the floor before I found the proper one. There it was! Everything was darkness except the round slab of rock where the sun hit the birthing table. Holding the picture under the light, I was able to see the face of Leah, highlighted on the left side. The face was six feet tall in relationship to the temple's slab. It was the same face I had seen as a child — my spirit lady.

"I can't believe it! Why didn't I see it before? You were the presence I felt. You really were there!"

"Not only was I present with you in the fertility temple, but I found great happiness in showing you our space station in Waynapicchu. All over your planet there are secret records of the Starseed Race that we will guide you to, for it is within your chosen destiny to bring this information to light for humanity. You have been coded in the DNA of your bloodstream to be able to handle these energies, and to carry and rediscover this ancient knowledge for your world. This is only the first step on that journey. Your personal myth will allow you to see that all facets of yourself — the light, the shadow, and the knowing — will heal you and make you whole."

"Where do I go next? What do I look for?" I questioned.

"*England — the only remaining portion of Atlantis above the sea. There you will find many of the secrets of the Starseed Race, and singing stones that will help you remember. We have left our marks and shall guide you. The dragon of wisdom sleeps there too — he awaits you. The dragon is an ancient symbol representing the breath of the creative force that is in all things. To look into the dragon's eyes is to be able to confront the wholeness of creation and your role in it. It is time for the full truth of humanity's history to be known. The process may be a long one and you must be certain that you are ready to handle the energy of the Vanished Ones.*"

"Leah, who are the Vanished Ones?"

"*The Vanished Ones are your planet's ancestors who came from the stars and helped to mold the destiny of this planet. Their records have been hidden for centuries, and contain certain energies that tell of their struggle against forces that would hide them forever in the hope that humanity would always be a race of slaves. You have uncovered a part of the myth of the race of gods and much of the history of those that served the light. Know that much more lies ahead. Every 25,000 years or so, the records were buried by great Earth changes when souls were harvested to move into the next dimension. Along with the wars you have already discovered, many vast civilizations were destroyed. You have come back to reclaim the history of the Vanished Ones. Know that we of the other realms will assist you. See us in the dragon's breath, the mists that create the veil between your world and ours. May our shining light be your guide as a reminder of your connection to the Force.*"

"But Leah, what if I don't find physical proof? Will I be made a fool of by the scientific communities of the world? You gave me the reflection of your face in the photo, and I have my notes and the artifacts, but I'm concerned about needing more."

"*Physical proof is never necessary. I chose to give you this photo as a gift. It is a token of my love. You are very hard on yourself. Do not deny the experiences you have had. Be at one with what is true for you. The darkness of your private storm has passed. Your song is to be sung. Find joy in the singing of it.*"

Leah was gone. As I sat and mused about what she had said, I saw the fires of that wedding feast in my other life, long ago. My name in that life came to me again—Midnight Song. The darkness of midnight had passed. I went to my typewriter and began to type. It was time for Midnight Song to sing.

— *About The Author* —

Jamie Sams is a trance channel, psychic archaeologist, and Native American medicine teacher who lives in Santa Fe, New Mexico. She is of Iroquois and Choctaw blood, and has been trained in the Seneca, Mayan, Aztec, and Choctaw traditions. She is also a member of the Seneca Wolf Clan.

Jamie has channelled extensively throughout the United States, as well as in seven foreign countries. Her association with Leah, the being whom she channels, has led her to ancient sites around the world in her search for information that will assist people on Earth to better understand their evolution as a planetary race. She has uncovered documentation implying that Earth has been visited by cultures from other planets in order to aid its biological and spiritual growth, and has appeared on radio and television to exhibit the artifacts and data she has retrieved.

Along with co-author David Carson, Jamie has also written *Medicine Cards: The Discovery of Power Through the Ways of Animals* (Bear & Co.), a system of divination using the teachings of animal medicine and the sacred traditions. As a medicine woman, her highest goal in life is to see the sacred teachings of the ages revealed, so that the name of the race of humanity will be "peace."

— *Tape Information* —

There are over 200 titles available on tape of Leah's channelled material. If you would like to receive more information on these tapes, write to:

LEAH/MIDNIGHT SONG
535 Cordova Road
Suite 430
Santa Fe, New Mexico 87501

YOUR BODY
YOUR UNIVERSE

A. The Atomic Garden Within

B. Organs and Emotions

C. Ridges, Dispersals, and Flows of Energy

D. Cellular Level Memory

E. Tools for Cleansing

F. Crystal Consciousness of the Seven Bodies

G. Being a Part of the Whole

H. Honoring Your Universe

I. The Spirit Within Foods

J. The Beauty of Spiritual Evolution

K. Divining the Divinity in You

L. Wholeness Achieved

PROFESSIONALLY- PRODUCED CASSETTES

1. Bioplasmic Universe & Intention

2. History of Crystals & Healing Uses

3. The Dream Reality

4. The Truth About Spirit

5. What Are Worthy Opponents?

6. Internal Dialogue: Mental Frequency Band .

7. The God Concept (2 tapes)

8. What is Power?

9. Black Hole Energy

10. Love: The Ultimate Physician

11. Personal History: These are the Good Old Days

12. Your Ageless Self

13. Solar Plexus Sensitivity

14. UFO's & Indian Power Places

15. The Effect You Create on the Universe & 4th D.